MW00625030

WANTED BY THE WOLF

The Nightstar Shifters 5

ARIEL MARIE

The first time I saw you, my heart whispered, "That's the one."

Unknown

Copyright © 2022 by Ariel Marie

Cover by Crimson Phoenix Creations.

Edited by Emmy Ellis with Studioenp.

This is a work of fiction. Names, characters, organizations, businesses, events, and incidents are a figment of the author's imagination and are used fictitiously. Any similarities to real people, businesses, locations, history, and events are a coincidence.

All rights reserved.

No part of this publication may be reproduced, distributed, or transmitted in any form or by any means, including photocopying, recording, or other electronic or mechanical methods, without the prior written permission of the publisher.

Paperback ISBN: 978-1-956602-14-2

CHAPTER ONE

"It's not too much longer," Skye said in her high singsong voice.

Her six-month-old son, Rolf, just wasn't taking that answer.

It had to be the third time she'd said the same thing.

Just a little longer and they would be at their destination.

His fussing calmed slightly. She glanced in the rearview mirror and caught sight of his bare chubby foot headed toward his mouth.

She bit back a chuckle. The boy always

managed to kick his socks off. She just didn't understand the fascination of putting one's foot in their mouth.

But if it was going to keep him from screaming bloody murder, then have at it.

Skye relaxed slightly in her seat and concentrated on the scene before her. There was nothing but open skies and road ahead of them. Her small sedan ate up the distance as she tested the engine. Her foot was a bit heavy on the gas pedal, but she had somewhere to be.

She and Rolf were on their way to make a new life for themselves. She was lucky to have escaped the clutches of her deranged father-in-law.

A shiver passed through her at the thought of that maniac. Her grip tightened on the steering wheel. A nervous breath escaped her. She flicked her gaze at the mirror and checked the road behind her.

Nothing.

The California highway was clear for the early Sunday morning trip. She had waited for the perfect moment to disappear from her small town of Half Moon Bay. It had been her home since she was a child, but now it was going to be a distant memory.

Howling Valley was her destination.

It was her hope and prayer that her son would be accepted amongst the Nightstar Pack. She had researched Howling Valley and the pack that had claimed it. From what she had learned, the Nightstar Pack had an alpha who was trustworthy and would help her.

He had to.

There was no way he would allow a woman on the run to continue on with her infant child.

Not with a monster like Barone Westway on her tail. She was sure every alpha in the state of California was familiar with Barone.

Her hands trembled at the thought of the large shifter taking her son away from her. What if this Evan Gerwulf was an ally to Barone? She couldn't imagine Barone would have many, but there was a slight possibility.

Was she unknowingly driving into a trap?

"No. Reade wouldn't have led me astray," she muttered. Her heart ached at the thought of her ex.

Reade Westway was a shifter who had been sweet on her. Skye had grown up amongst the shifters of her town, and she was very familiar with their ways. She had long known that she wasn't

Reade's mate, but he had insisted on pursuing her anyway.

He had been kind, and she was unsure how he was the son of the alpha who ruled their local pack. Skye was naturally shy and had been taken aback that the wolf with warm eyes had been interested in her.

Skye's lips curled up into a smile when she thought of the first time he'd approached her. She had been waiting tables, and every night she worked, he had dined in her area.

Their friendship began, and before long she found their relationship moving to the next level. Skye knew what they had wouldn't last, but Reade was stubborn and claimed he didn't care about finding his mate. He wanted to be with her.

But that was not the way of wolves.

Barone did not accept that his son had stooped so low to court a human. He wanted his son to mate with one of their own and rule at his side then take over the pack.

The alpha had much on his hands with the unrest of his own people. He was challenged multiple times for his seat. The town had become dangerous. The humans afraid for their lives.

In Half Moon Bay, a civil war soon broke out. It

was all too much. The war had spilled out into the town.

There were human and shifter casualties.

Her son's father was one of them.

Not trusting Barone, she grabbed her son and ran.

Skye blinked and almost missed the sign on the edge of the road.

Howling Valley.

They had arrived. She pressed down on the pedal to speed up her little car. Now they were in Howling Valley, Barone wouldn't have any pull in this town. This wasn't his territory.

There were laws shifters were to abide by.

Reade had once mentioned this town, and even he had thought to bring them here.

"Finally." She took the next exit and could have wept.

They had made it.

Now she had to follow shifter laws.

When a shifter was in a territory not their own, they had to inform the leaders of their business.

Even though Skye wasn't a shifter, her son was, and she didn't want to chance the wrath of the new alpha by not following the laws.

Soon she was driving down a long winding

road. Her GPS directing her to the home of the Nightstar Pack's alpha.

A large house with a wraparound porch came into a view. Skye parked at the edge of the drive and killed the engine. Her hands trembled with the fear of the unknown.

"Keep your anxiety down," she murmured.

Wolves could scent fear and any emotions. That was a painful experience she'd learned.

The front door opened, and a short female exited the house. She looked to be in her mid-forties, but Skye understood that shifters stopped aging at one point in their lives.

The woman stopped at the edge of the stairs and had a welcoming smile on her face.

Skye exhaled.

"Now or never," she announced. Rolf's babble was the only response. She turned around and peeked at him. Now both of his feet were free from his socks. "Come on, baby boy."

She got out of the car and took Rolf out. He squealed and held on to her shirt. She took his diaper bag out and rested the strap on her shoulder. Shutting the door to the car, she walked around to the front.

"Hello there," the woman called out.

"Hello. I'm Skye, and this is Rolf." Skye walked over to the porch and stopped at the foot of the stairs.

"I'm Jena. Welcome to Howling Valley. How can I help you?"

Jena Gerwulf. Skye relaxed as she returned the woman's smile. Rolf reached out and waved his fingers at the alpha's mate.

He didn't appear scared at all by her. The baby had a way of detecting a person's character. It must be his shifter genes.

"I'm wanting to relocate here. I've heard great things about the town and um…" She paused and glanced at her son. She was here for him. She had to be truthful with them if she were to request their permission to settle in their town with her tiny shifter son. "My son is a shifter, and we need help."

Jena's smile disappeared. Her gaze darted to Rolf. She inhaled sharply then gave Skye a nod.

"Come in, dear. Evan, my mate, is home."

Skye tightened her hold of Rolf. She walked up the stairs and followed the wolf inside her home. The vibe she was getting was that of a house where it was lived-in and welcoming. Photos were placed with who Skye assumed were family members and grandchildren.

She passed by a few men scattered throughout the structure who appeared to be enforcers.

Skye was familiar with the hierarchy of wolves. Reade had been an enforcer for this father.

They entered the living room where Jena ushered her over to the couch.

"My mate should be here in a moment. Can I get you something to drink? A snack?" Jena asked, taking the seat on the couch that faced Skye's.

"I'm good. Just tired. We've driven a long way, and I'm just looking forward to being able to lie down and sleep." She smiled sheepishly.

Heavy footsteps carried down the hall outside the room, and soon a tall, broad-shouldered man with dark hair came in.

The air around him screamed alpha. His laser-sharp gaze landed on her. She stiffened slightly.

This was not Barone.

She'd heard plenty about Evan Gerwulf.

Reade had mentioned this pack and was confident this alpha would be fair and honorable.

Too bad Reade hadn't been able to come with them.

"Who do we have here?" Evan asked. He stalked over to his wife and stood behind the couch.

"Come sit down, Evan. You're scaring her." Jena motioned for him to sit next to her.

So much for Skye trying to keep her fear down.

Jena's nose must be extra sensitive.

The alpha didn't put up a protest but moved over and settled beside his mate. His long legs were stretched out in front of him.

"Hello, sir. My name is Skye Lennon, and this is my son, Rolf Westway."

"Westway?" Evan's eyebrows rose. Curiosity filled his gaze. He sat forward and rested his forearms on his knees. "Any relation to Barone Westway?"

Skye swallowed hard and exhaled. Her shoulders slumped at the realization she wouldn't have been able to hide who she or her son were.

Not that she wanted to.

She'd had thoughts of not using her son's real last name, but she didn't want to be dishonest.

"Yes, my son's father was Reade Westway, the son of Barone Westway."

Jena's sharp intake of breath was the only sound in the room. Evan stared at her momentarily then moved his gaze to her son. Rolf, sitting on her lap, turned his head, his eyes connecting with the alpha's.

Skye's hands grew moist. She rubbed them on her jeans and waited.

"I'm sorry to hear of your mate's passing." Evan leaned back, resting his arm along the back of the couch.

"We weren't mated." Skye cleared her throat. "But thank you."

"Why are you here?" Evan asked.

His facial expression was unreadable, and Skye's nervousness was increasing rapidly.

"After Reade passed away, I just wanted a new start and I heard Howling Valley was a great place to raise a child. I wanted Rolf to be around good wolves and have a stable environment."

"And this didn't have anything to do with the war I heard that broke out in Half Moon Bay or that Barone has been on a rampage searching for his heir?"

Skye froze in place. She tried to hold the alpha's hard gaze but couldn't. Her gaze dropped to the floor.

"Please don't send me away. I'm willing to do whatever I have to in order to stay," she whispered.

As if sensing his mother's emotions, Rolf leaned into her and sighed.

"Evan," Jena snapped.

"What?" Evan turned to his mate.

"Don't be so hard on her." She glared at him.

Skye was impressed. Her father-in-law wouldn't have stood for anyone talking to him in that manner.

Not even his own mate.

"It's okay, ma'am. If we aren't allowed to stay, all I ask is just a night to rest and we'll be on our way." Skye hadn't been prepared for this. If she couldn't stay, then she would have to figure out something else. There was another town over in Arizona she could go to. Maybe they would help her.

Ideas flew in her mind. She'd have to fill up on gas, grab something to eat. To save money, they could sleep in the car—

"Nonsense." The alpha's low grumble cut into her thoughts.

Skye blinked and found the alpha staring at her.

"I know Barone and how dangerous he is. I'm sure he will be hunting that baby down, and there is no way I can just sit back and allow him to take that child from you."

Tears blurred Skye's vision. She inhaled a shaky breath and tightened her grip around Rolf.

"Thank you, sir. You're correct. He wants my

son and couldn't give a damn about me. I will do whatever I must to keep him safe. I can't have him grow up in the environment his father did."

"You can stay here in Howling Valley. You and the child are welcome." Evan glanced at his mate who was beaming at him. His facial features softened slightly.

Skye would kill to be able to have that with someone. It didn't take a shifter to see these two were meant to be together. Jena patted Evan on the chest, then they both turned to her.

"I really appreciate this. I am willing to contribute to the pack and carry my weight."

"Don't worry." Evan held up his hand. "It won't be safe for now. I will try to reason with Barone on your behalf, but I expect a fight to come out of this."

"No." She jumped to her feet. She shifted Rolf around onto her hip. Another fight or war was what she was trying to avoid. "I can't ask that of you. I wouldn't want anyone to get hurt because of us. I'll figure something else out."

"Stay." The alpha's voice was low and unthreatening.

Rolf paused his wiggling in her arms as if his

own little animal detected the alpha's beast was nearby.

"Your best option is here with the Nightstar wolves. We will offer you protection and a safe place to stay."

CHAPTER TWO

"You all should be proud of yourselves," a deep voice rang out.

Ricca Radcliff stood to her full height. She held her chin up high as pride filled her.

She had finally fulfilled a long-time dream.

Now, she was an official enforcer for the Nightstar Pack. It had been hard work, and she had persevered.

She peeked down the line with the other wolves who stood beside her. They had grown close through their training and trials to complete the requirements to work underneath their alpha and protect their pack.

From the time she was a pup, Ricca had known she wanted to join the ranks of enforcer. She had admired her older cousin, Decker, who had been like an idol to her. She didn't have any siblings, but that didn't bother her one bit. Her family was close, and her cousins filled the void. Decker had joined the enforcers when she was in high school. He was about ten years older than her and was senior enforcer.

It wasn't too long ago she had been working in her stuffy office in cyber security. Decker had called her and shared with her they were looking for wolves to join the enforcers and specifically a few females.

Sitting behind a desk all day just wasn't for her. Her wolf was dying for some action.

It was as if the gods above knew what was in her heart.

Protecting people was her calling. She was good at her previous job, but this was something she was destined for.

The Nightstar Pack was one of the most well-known packs in all of the state, and their enforcers were one of the toughest out there. The training was rigorous, but Ricca had been determined to make it.

Today was the day they were made official. She glanced over to where the families and public were seated watching the ceremony. Her gaze landed on her parents, Roger and Cinder, who smiled and waved to her. Cinder had tears streaming down her face. Ricca grinned at them curiously, taking in who else from the town was there.

It was a small gathering, and important members of their community were there to witness the pinning of the new enforcers.

She was met with the intense gaze of the alpha, Evan Gerwulf. He gave her a nod, turning his attention away. He was seated in the front row with his mate and the beta's mate.

That look meant everything.

She glanced back over where Mick, the beta, was giving a speech.

"It is important to remember what it means to be a member of a strong team. We wanted the best our pack had to give us, and it was you." He waved his hand toward them.

Ricca peeked at the others and was met by the gaze of the only other female to make it this year.

Ginger was cool and had grown up in Howling Valley. Through their training they had stuck together. There weren't that many female enforcers around, and they had grown close. They had to make sure they were better than the guys to even make the team.

Mick completed his speech and stepped down for the pinning ceremony. He stopped in front of each recruit. It didn't take long before he made his way to her.

"Ricca Radcliff. I should have known you'd make it. You are one stubborn wolf, and I'm proud of you. The cyber team has lost a great person, but the pack will be in good hands with you as an enforcer." He took her jacket and gently applied her pin to it.

"Thank you, sir. I won't let you down," she said. Her wolf whined slightly, bowing her head. She sensed the beta's beast and was ready to submit to him.

"I know you won't." He gave her a nod and moved on to the next person.

Ricca gazed down at her bright shiny gold pin that was resting on her chest. This was a tradition for those who had completed the training and approved for the job to receive not only the symbol of their pack, but an official uniform that denoted her position in the pack.

"To the citizens of Howling Valley, I now present to you the new members of your protectors," Mick announced.

Applause thundered around them.

The ceremony was over.

"Congratulations." Armel, who had been posted next to her, turned and held out his hand.

"Thanks." She grinned and took his hand in a firm grip.

A few others in their group surrounded them. Laughter filled the air. There were a few candidates who hadn't made it, and the seven of them were all that was left from their class. In the months they had to work together, they had grown close. They were going to have to continue to work close together along with the older members of the enforcement team.

"My baby!"

Ricca turned around to find her parents racing toward her. She gave a wave to her team. "I'll see you guys later."

She met her parents who immediately brought her in for hugs and kisses.

"Hey, Ma." Ricca laughed.

Her mother's arms were tight around her. Cinder was known to be overly dramatic. Both Roger and Ricca knew how she was, and they adored her. In her animal form, Cinder was a fierce wolf who was highly protective of her family.

"I'm so proud of you." Cinder laughed. She planted another kiss on Ricca's cheek and released her.

"My turn," her father grumbled. He snagged Ricca's hand and brought her into his embrace.

She leaned into it, loving how her parents were always supportive of her.

"Hey, Dad." Ricca squeezed him tight then let go.

"We are so proud of you," Cinder said. She wiped her cheeks and smiled. "Why don't you come over to the house and I'll cook dinner for us. I already told Decker to tell everyone to come."

The Radcliffs were a large, close-knit family. Ricca may not have had any siblings, but there was never a day she was lonely, thanks to all of her cousins. Her father and his five brothers ensured that.

"Sure, Mom. That sounds great." Ricca's wolf sat up at the mention of her mother's cooking.

Cinder was a fabulous cook, and it was a wonder that Ricca and Roger weren't overweight.

"Roger. Cinder. Ricca." The alpha's deep voice startled Ricca. He and his mate, Jena, stood beside them.

"Alpha." Her father stepped toward him with his hand outstretched.

Cinder and Jena shared a hug.

"Alpha. Jena." Ricca bowed her head to them.

"I'm glad you finally came to your senses to leave that company and come work for the pack." Evan's lips curled up into a smile. He had been trying to recruit her to come work for his family's boating company for years, but continuing in cyber security hadn't been her long-term goal.

"I figured working for the pack was the right move to make in my career," she joked.

"You two have raised a fine young woman," Evan announced, resting a hand on her shoulder.

"We did our best." Her father sighed and ran a hand through his hair.

She didn't miss the growing twinkle in his eyes. "Dad!" She nudged him with her elbow. She had been the perfect kid they could have asked for. She had always had straight A's in school and had graduated at the top of her class in college. "I'm thirty-two years old, not a teenager."

"It doesn't matter how old you are, you are still our child." Cinder's hand skated along her back.

"Do you mind if I steal her away for a moment?" the alpha asked.

Ricca's eyebrows flew up in shock. Her parents gave a nod and turned to Jena.

"Have I done something wrong?" Ricca asked, walking alongside Evan.

"Not at all." Evan chuckled. He led them away from the crowd.

Ricca's curiosity was piqued.

What could the alpha want with her?

"The one thing about becoming an enforcer, one must be ready at any time for me to call with a job," he began. The smile was gone from his lips, and before her stood the intense alpha they had all come to trust with their pack.

"Sir." Ricca beat down her excitement. Was the alpha about to hand her her first assignment?

"We have a situation of a woman who has moved here with her young child. Her son is the heir to a powerful alpha who is very dangerous. She has come to Howling Valley to seek refuge."

Ricca was all ears. Even her animal grew still and was paying attention.

"What I need is someone I can trust to guard this woman and her child with their life. She's scared and on the run."

Ricca gave a slight nod to confirm she was listening.

"I need someone I can count on who will keep them safe while we deal with her old alpha and pack. This would be a private duty case, and I'm entrusting the safety of this woman and her child to you."

"Yes, sir. Thank you for thinking of me for this. I won't let you down." She was curious on why the alpha was willing to take on another pack, but it wasn't her place to question him.

"She's staying at my house. We will assign a safe house for you to take her to. I'm hoping this situation will be handled within the week. I want everyone to make her feel safe and welcomed. She hasn't shared much with me, but I can tell she's been through a lot."

Ricca had grown up in Howling Valley, and it was a wonderful town to live in and raise a family. She would make sure this woman and child felt comfortable in their town. She couldn't imagine having to be on the run to protect a child.

Ricca would not let them down. This was her first job, and she would prove she could handle anything thrown at her.

Her wolf stood and paced impatiently. It would seem they both were on the same page. No woman or child would ever have to fear for their lives under their protection.

"When should I pick her up?"

CHAPTER THREE

"You just don't want to nap, do you?" Skye grinned at her son who was propped up on the pillows on the bed. She was busy packing their bags so they could go with the escort who would be protecting them. She was nervous to meet the enforcer who was assigned to them. She didn't want to be a burden and she would ensure she followed any instructions the enforcer issued to keep her and Rolf safe.

"I'm sure they are just going to love being a babysitter to us," Skye muttered. She slid Rolf's clothing in his bag and zipped it shut.

Rolf's giggle snagged her attention.

She stuck her tongue out at him, eliciting more of his laughter. She smiled and shook her head. Her little wolf was growing up so fast. It was a shame his father would never get to see him become a man or an adult wolf. Reade would have made a good father to Rolf. She wasn't sure if they would have remained together or not. As much as he'd assured her he didn't want anyone else, the thought that his true mate would show up one day had always sat in the back of her head.

As a shifter, he wouldn't have been able to control his animal.

Barone would have done anything in his power to separate them. She shivered at the thought of her father-in-law. He was a mean wolf and he always wanted to prove his power.

Skye, a mere human, would have been no match for him.

Her gaze fell on Rolf, and she knew *she* would do anything in *her* power to keep her son from his grandfather.

Jena had shared with her that they would be safe here in Howling Valley.

So far, it was the safest she had felt in a long time.

Last night was the first time she'd gotten a full night's rest.

Even her greedy little son hadn't woken up demanding to be fed.

Rolf squealed and reached for her. She picked up one of his toys and handed it to him.

"I need to finish packing, sir." She tossed him a grin and scurried around the room throwing the rest of her clothes into her duffle bag. She didn't want to make the enforcer wait when he arrived. Rolf took his plush toy and gnawed on it.

Skye grimaced at the memory of him doing the same to her boob. Her poor baby was teething and chewed on anything he could get his hands on. His four teeth he had were small, but they hurt like hell.

Skye placed their bags on the bed and stood back, resting her hands on her waist. A quick glance revealed the room was as clean as when they'd first entered last night.

A knock sounded at the door.

"Come in," Skye called out. She walked around the bed toward Rolf who dropped his toy and reached out for her. She hefted him up and rested him against her body.

"Are you all packed?" Jena stepped into the

room. Her warm-eyed gaze landed on Rolf, and a grin spread across her face.

Her baby had this effect on everyone. He always brought a smile to anyone who met him.

"Yes, we are." Skye nodded.

"Your escort is here. Come, I'll help you with your bags." Jena picked up the bags and moved toward the door.

"Jena, I just want to let you know that I appreciate everything you are doing for us." Skye grabbed Rolf's toy and followed behind Jena.

"Oh, don't you worry about it. We could never turn away a woman and her child. Evan will make everything right." Jena strolled down the hall toward the stairway.

The home was large and homey. Skye was envious of their house and hoped one day she would own something close. Not that it had to be large, but she could feel the love in the air. She prayed she would find someone who would love her and her son.

She should be thinking of meeting someone, but it would be nice to find someone who understood her, could love her, and accept her son.

One step at a time, Skye.

She inhaled and followed the alpha's mate down

the steps. She had plenty of time to daydream, but first the issue of her deranged father-in-law was still hanging over her head…

"Ouch!" Skye laughed. Rolf had a handful of her hair and was tugging on her strands. She untangled his fingers from her thick locks. His grip was strong. She made it to the bottom of the stairs. His laughter filled the air. Apparently, tugging on his mother's hair was funny. "Don't snatch me bald, baby."

"Oh, I remember when my children were that age. My hair was always a target." Jenna chuckled.

Skye managed to free herself from the clutches of her little wolf.

"He loves playing in my hair." Skye shook her head and followed the older woman through the house. They arrived at the family room and found the alpha and their son, Conon.

Conon, the eldest child of the Gerwulfs, was almost identical to his father. He was tall and broad-shouldered with the same intense eyes and dark hair. He had stopped by last night and ate dinner with them. Rolf had taken to him right away.

"There he is." Conon smiled at Rolf who squealed and waved his little fingers at the large wolf.

"Oh my goodness. He waved!" Skye gasped.

Skye's heart warmed at the reception of this family to her and her child. It amazed her how her son could pick up that these people were good. The few times he had been around his grandfather, he'd screamed and cried, not wanting Barone to touch him.

Here, around the Gerwulfs, he wanted to be around them.

This just solidified that moving to Howling Valley was the right thing to do. She wanted him to grow up around wolves who could be a role model to him. From everything she could tell from the alpha and his son, they were good men.

Skye had done her research on this family, and the Gerwulfs were richer beyond any means she had ever known. Their boating company was world-renowned. Their pack was one of the strongest in the west. Unfortunately, her old pack was not weak by any means. They were strong and ferocious. She worried that Barone would not see reason to whatever Evan would present to him.

"His wolf will be a strong one," Conon proclaimed. He went over to them and held out his finger to Rolf who took it.

Skye beamed at the announcement. It was as if

Conon had sensed her worries. He ruffled Rolf's hair, walking over to his father's side.

A movement behind Conon caught Skye's eye. She hadn't seen the newcomer who must have been blocked by the size of the alpha's son.

The woman was tall with hair so light, it was almost white.

She was definitely a wolf.

Her amber eyes gave it away. She was toned, and it was apparent she worked out, or it was just that she was a shifter.

Skye wasn't sure why her heart stuttered when their eyes met.

"Skye, allow me to introduce to you to Ricca Radcliff. She is the enforcer assigned to protect you and Rolf," Evan said.

This woman was an enforcer?

Skye had never heard of such a thing. Back home in Half Moon Bay, there weren't any female enforcers. Barone wouldn't have allowed it. Not that there weren't good women in the pack, he just didn't believe a woman should hold that type of job.

"Hello." Ricca's husky voice broke Skye from her thoughts. She strode forward and held out her hand.

"Um, hi. I'm Skye," Skye stammered. She took

the wolf's hand and gasped. A warm sensation traveled up her arm instantly. She let go of her, but her fingers were still tingling from the woman's touch.

She almost took a step back away from her.

What the hell was that?

She glanced down at Rolf who had grown silent and was watching Ricca. The enforcer's gaze dropped to Rolf and immediately softened.

"Oh my! He's such a cutie," Ricca exclaimed.

Rolf offered her a grin, and he quickly won over the enforcer.

Her little son was becoming a woman magnet.

"Thank you," Skye said softly. She had yet to take her eyes off the woman. She had never had this reaction to anyone before. Her heart sped up as Ricca's eyes flicked to hers.

"Ricca will be escorting you to a private cabin and will protect you from there until everything blows over," Evan said.

Skye tore her eyes from Ricca and focused on the alpha.

She was going to be alone with this woman in a secluded cabin?

Just the two of them?

Well, not just the two of them. Rolf would be there, too.

Skye cleared her throat and jerked her head in a nod. It wasn't up to her to question the alpha. If he thought the best thing was for her to stay with Ricca, then that was what she would do. Her main goal was to keep Rolf safe and with her.

Hidden away with a gorgeous woman was going to be the least of her worries.

She glanced back at Ricca and swallowed hard. The wolf's amber eyes were locked on her with an intensity that took her breath away.

Okay, maybe not the least of her worries.

"Don't worry. We'll stay out of sight, allow the pack to work things out with your old one, and you'll be free to go soon." Ricca smiled at her, and again, Skye's heart skipped a beat.

What was it about this wolf?

"Should I follow you in my car?" Skye asked. She bounced Rolf on her hip to quiet him down. His babbling was growing in urgency.

"We're going to put your car up in storage. We wouldn't want anyone recognizing it should someone be looking for you." Evan motioned for them to follow him.

Conon grabbed her bags from the doorway, and they all exited the home. A black SUV was parked out front of the house.

Jena and Ricca took Rolf's car seat over to her truck while Conon loaded the bags in the back. Skye had him move over the other things that had been stored away in her trunk.

"I have a scheduled call with Barone and I'm sure he will resist at first." Evan stood next to Skye. He towered over her.

She tilted her head back to meet his gaze.

"I'm sure he's not going to take kindly that I'm intervening, but it is only what is right. He cannot make you give up your baby to him. Not in the human world, nor the shifters'."

"I trust your decision," Skye admitted.

Rolf leaned into her, resting his head against her chest.

She ran a hand along his back and pressed a kiss to her head. Whatever she had to do to keep this little guy safe, she would do. "Whatever you think is best."

"We're ready." Ricca marched over to them. She gave a nod to the alpha. "Sir, again, thank you for the honor."

"You don't have to thank me. You are the right fit for this job." He patted Ricca on the shoulder then walked back to the house and met Jena on the porch.

Skye stared at the SUV and inhaled.

"Are you ready?" Ricca asked.

"As I'll ever be." Skye followed Ricca to the truck.

Once Rolf was secured in his seat, they were on their way. Skye watched the Gerwulfs' house in the side mirror as it grew smaller off in the distance.

She inhaled and rested back in her chair while Ricca drove them down the long dirt road.

Everything was going to be okay.

It had to be.

They drove for a while in silence. Skye stared out the window, taking in the breathtaking view of the woods surrounding them. She could certainly get used to Howling Valley. It was a beautiful town, and she couldn't wait to explore it and see all it had to offer.

"You don't have to be afraid," Ricca's voice broke the silence in the truck. There was a frown on the wolf's face as she let her window down.

Skye studied her for a moment. Her long hair whipped around in the wind from the open window. She was a stunning woman, and Skye just couldn't get an understanding of her reaction to her.

"I'm not," she admitted with a sigh. She reached up and tucked her hair behind her ear. It was warm outside today, and it was the type of day she wouldn't mind sitting out on the porch of her old home and sipping on a nice cup of iced tea.

"I can scent your fear. It's almost stifling." Ricca glanced over at her briefly, turning her attention back to the road.

"I guess it's just the unknown that I'm worried about." Skye shrugged.

"Don't worry. I will protect you and your son." Ricca reached over and took Skye's hand and gave it a quick squeeze. "This I promise you."

Skye couldn't respond. She stared down at their entwined fingers. Ricca released her, and Skye couldn't stop looking at her hand.

She wasn't sure why, but she had her full trust in the Nightstar Pack.

She had a feeling that they stuck by their word and would do everything in their power to ensure she and Rolf would be free from Barone and his minions.

They fell back into a comfortable silence with light rock playing on the radio.

She hadn't missed the way Ricca clenched the steering wheel.

Something was bothering the wolf.

Too bad she didn't have the abilities like the

wolves to sense emotions or scents.

Was the enforcer upset she was stuck babysitting her and Rolf? Was she wanting to get in on whatever action that might occur when dealing with her father-in-law?

Skye reminded herself that she was a job for this woman. The wolf was trying to comfort her, and all she could think of was taking Ricca's hand and sliding it down into her jeans...

Skye blinked.

No, ma'am. This wasn't what she was supposed to be thinking about.

She would ignore all the hints of an attraction she had for her. That warm, tingling sensation that raced up her arm when they first shook hands.

It was all in her imagination. It had to be the stress of being on the run. She was going to have to ignore what she thought was there.

No matter how much her core clenched at the thought of Ricca kissing her.

Nope, she wouldn't imagine that at all.

Stop it, Skye.

She would die of embarrassment if Ricca mentioned the scent of her arousal.

She clenched her thighs together and prayed the cabin was close by.

CHAPTER FOUR

Ricca's grip tightened on the steering wheel. The scent of Skye's arousal was tempting her. Her gums burned and stretched from her fangs descending. The sweet tanginess of Skye's wetness was calling to her. She licked her lips, wanting to take the woman and spread her out on the ground and bury her face between her legs. The aroma was growing stronger, and it took everything Ricca had to not growl.

She didn't want to scare the woman.

Her wolf paced at the thought of Skye being afraid. Neither her beast nor Ricca liked the thought of Skye being afraid of anything.

Ricca focused her attention on the road. The cabin wasn't too far away. She just had to get them there and inside, then she'd shift and check out the perimeter.

Ricca had everything to prove to her alpha. She wanted to meet his expectations. He had chosen her for this job, and she was not going to let him down.

She inhaled and sharply exhaled. From the moment her gaze had landed on the beautiful woman carrying her baby, her wolf had gone crazy. She'd tried to claw her way out of Ricca's abdomen, demanding to shift and go to her. When they'd stood in the alpha's home, the scent of this woman drifted over to her, and she knew immediately Skye was meant for her.

Ricca's wolf had never responded to anyone like this before. It was only one reason why her wolf would be losing her mind.

Skye was her mate.

This, she was sure.

Ricca breathed in again, and the raw need to taste Skye was consuming her. She pressed her foot down on the gas pedal. If she didn't get them to the cabin soon, she wouldn't be responsible for her actions.

"Is everything all right?" Skye's soft voice broke through Ricca's thoughts.

Ricca jerked her head around and took in Skye staring at her. Her wide brown eyes were curiously taking Ricca in.

"Yes." Ricca cleared her throat. "I'm fine. Why?"

"You look as if you are about to rip the steering wheel off and you keep growling."

Ricca cursed and tried to relax in her seat. She offered an awkward smile at Skye. She turned her attention back to the road.

"I'm good. My wolf is impatient and ready to go for a run," Ricca lied. Her heart skipped a beat at the lie. Even little Ricca didn't want to lie to Skye.

Mate.

The one word was whispered in the back of her mind, and she knew what it was.

Her animal proclaiming what she already knew.

She wasn't sure of how much Skye knew of their kind. Seeing how her child was half human and half shifter, Ricca would assume Skye knew something. Jealousy filled Ricca.

Where was the baby's father?

Why wasn't he here to protect her?

Within minutes she was guiding the truck to the cabin. It was a small, one-bedroom home that was reserved for private guests of the alpha. Their compound was filled with plenty of cabins and homes.

She parked the vehicle in the spot in front of the home. There was no garage, and the house was surrounded by lush forest.

Ricca's wolf couldn't wait to stretch her legs and explore the area.

But first they had to get Skye and baby Rolf inside the house.

"Let me go check it out to make sure everything is okay." Ricca killed the engine and exited the vehicle. She went inside the home and walked around. The single bedroom would be reserved for Skye and Rolf. Ricca would take the couch. It looked comfortable and was long enough to fit her five-foot-nine frame with no problem.

After a quick sweep through the rest of the cabin, she made her way outside to Skye.

"Everything good?" Skye asked, stepping out of the truck.

"Yeah." Ricca opened the trunk so she could grab their bags while Skye attended to Rolf. She shut the door and made a mental note to come back to get the rest of the items they had moved from Skye's car to her truck and her own duffle bag. "I can give you the grand tour then I need to do a quick perimeter check."

"Lead the way," Skye joked, a twinkle appearing in her eyes.

Rolf leaned against her chest and held on. The little wolf must have dozed off on the ride here.

Was Skye flirting with her?

Ricca froze.

She had to get a hold of herself. Maybe she was just being nice. They were going to be roommates after all, and her safety was dependent on Ricca.

Ricca offered her a smile and motioned for her to follow behind her.

They went inside with Skye walking around. Ricca carried Skye's bags into the bedroom and sat them on the large king bed. She inhaled sharply and tried to get control of her animal.

Her wolf was going crazy.

Mate.

This was not the time for her wolf to find her mate. This was a job. Her first one after becoming an enforcer, and she couldn't fail.

She didn't even want to know if the alpha found out she was pining after her charge.

Once she got her animal to calm down, she went back to the living room and met Skye who was coming out of the kitchen.

"I'm going to go outside and check out the property, then I'll grab the rest of your items from the truck."

"Okay." Skye smiled at her while she bounced Rolf up and down in her arms.

The baby turned and met her gaze. His amber eyes glowed, and she sensed his pup inside him. Her animal wanted to get closer to him and breathe in his scent. She was pulled toward him, and she wasn't sure why, but she felt a strong protective urge when she was around him.

"This is much nicer than I had imagined," Skye said.

"Good." Ricca backed away from Skye, afraid she would reach out and bring her into her arms. She spun around on her heels and headed outside. Her animal pushed against her stomach, wanting to be let out. She wanted to run around, but now wasn't the time to play.

Ricca took her time and strolled around the building. No strange scents. The yard looked undisturbed. She glanced around and didn't see anything in the area.

Her animal whined, begging for her to shift and let her out.

"Not now," Ricca murmured. "I promise later you can run free."

Satisfied, she went back to the truck and took out the contraption called a pack-and-play. She slammed the trunk shut and went back into the cabin. She wasn't sure what it was. Ricca knew nothing of children and the things they needed. Apparently, it was something Skye felt she needed. She had made sure Ricca had taken it out of her car to bring it with them.

The bed was big enough for Skye to share with the baby.

Ricca carried the thing to the master bedroom. She froze in the doorway.

Skye was sitting on the bed breastfeeding the baby.

Ricca didn't want to intrude on the intimate moment. She began to back away, but Skye's head snapped in her direction.

"Hey," Skye greeted her with a smile. She waved her in. "You can place that over there in the corner. I can guide you through how to set it up. It's not hard to do."

"What is this?" Ricca asked. It took a little

coaxing before she could get her feet to move. She swallowed hard and tried to not take another peek at Skye. The soft creamy skin of her breast could be seen above Rolf's head, his small hand resting along the curve of her breast while he fed from her.

"It's a portable bed for the baby." Skye giggled.

Ricca tried to avert her eyes, but she couldn't stop staring at Skye.

"I'm a wild sleeper, and Rolfie will need his own bed. He takes after me, and we will fight over this bed."

Ricca chuckled. She didn't want to begin to imagine Skye lying in the bed. When she did, the image of the naked human had her core clenching. Her breath caught in her throat. The small glimpse of her smooth skin was already causing Ricca's body to overheat. Her wolf paced back and forth inside her. The animal was pissed that she wasn't allowed to be let out so she could go over to Skye.

Skye gave Ricca some instructions to construct the baby's bed. They were surprisingly easy, and within minutes she had it put together and ready. Stepping back, she smiled, happy she was able to do this for Skye. It was a square contraption that would appear to keep the baby safe and allow him to sleep alone.

She glanced over at Skye, and her gaze was drawn to her bare breast again. Her rosy nipple was exposed while she switched Rolf over to her other mound. Ricca's hands trembled, and she fought to keep her feet still and not take a step toward Skye. The sweet scent of her milk reached Ricca.

Her wolf threw her head back and howled.

The urge to go to her and take the vacated place at her bare breast was strong.

"Are you hungry? I'm going to go make us some sandwiches," Ricca said abruptly. She flew out of the room, not even waiting for a response from Skye.

She had to put some distance between them. The cabin was stocked with the basics. She would take Skye out to the grocery store so she could pick out food she may want. It would do them some good to get some fresh air and go into town. She wasn't sure how long she would be able to keep herself from acting on these urges.

RICCA SHUT the fridge and turned back to the two plates resting on the counter. Now that she had put

some room between her and Skye, she was beginning to think more clearly.

She grabbed a bag of chips and poured some
on each of the plates next to the cold-cut sandwiches she had made. Ricca bit her lip and hoped
Skye would enjoy the simple meal.

The scent of lilacs was drawing closer. Without
turning around, she sensed Skye approaching. Her
light floral aroma was a dead giveaway.

Her wolf would recognize the scent anywhere.

"Have I done something to upset you?" Skye
asked.

Ricca jerked around to find her propped against
the doorjamb. Ricca was slightly disappointed to
find Skye had replaced her clothes and was not
walking around with her breasts exposed. They
were currently hidden by her soft t-shirt. Ricca bit
back a snort at that fantasy.

"No, not at all." Ricca shook her head. She
leaned back against the counter. "Why would you
think that?"

"Well, your wolf keeps growling whenever I'm
around you. I know I'm not a wolf, but that can't be
normal." Skye shrugged. A strange look passed
across her face. "I'm sort of used to wolves growling
at me who didn't like me."

Ricca frowned. How couldn't someone like her? She strode forward until she stopped directly in front of Skye. She left a hair's breadth of room between them. She reached out and took Skye's hand in hers.

"It's not directed at you," Ricca admitted.

"I'm sure you would rather be somewhere else than babysitting me and Rolf." Skye sighed.

"Actually, no. This job is an honor. I was chosen by the alpha to protect you and your son. If my alpha felt you were priority, then I will protect you as he has wished."

"Really?" Skye's eyebrows rose sharply. She continued to study Ricca for a few more moments before she relaxed slightly.

"Yes. I don't question the alpha. Apparently, he felt I was the best candidate for the job. He could have chosen any of the enforcers, but he picked me."

Ricca was going to have to get her animal together. She couldn't afford to have Skye thinking she didn't like her when it was absolutely the furthest from the truth. She wanted Skye to feel welcome while she figured out how to share with her that she was her mate.

And she would tell her, but she wanted to make

sure Skye would understand. She wasn't sure what had happened between her and the wolf shifter who'd fathered Rolf, but they could not have been mates because Skye belonged to her.

She gave Skye's hand a squeeze and stepped back before she did something like kiss her. Ricca's gaze dropped down to Skye's plump lips.

It was so tempting.

As if sensing her attention, Skye's lips parted. Her tongue snuck out and ran along her bottom lip, wetting it. Ricca inhaled sharply. Her gaze flicked to Skye's. Her bedroom-brown eyes were locked on Ricca.

"Well, I'm glad that you don't hate me or anything." A shaky laugh escaped Skye. She moved closer to Ricca and leaned back to the counter.

"What? How could I hate you?" Ricca's wolf paced back and forth. She whined, wanting to assure Skye.

"Believe me, I'm used to wolves not liking me." A strange look appeared in her eyes. It disappeared just as quick as it came. Skye's eyes grew unfocused as she stared off into space.

"Why?"

Sky jumped at the harshness of Ricca's question. Ricca closed the gap between them and took

Skye by the shoulders. Her wolf was ready to break free to protect their mate. She didn't want to think of someone not liking Skye or wanting to do her harm. From the feeling she sensed, Ricca picked up there was more to the story than what she knew.

Skye's sad eyes met Ricca's. Her lips trembled when they parted. She blinked a few times and looked away from Ricca.

"Back home, many of the wolves didn't want me to have a relationship with my ex," she began. She reached up and brushed her hair from her face. Her lips curled up in the corner in a sarcastic grin. "But honestly, I don't think that truly mattered. I think it was just me."

Ricca drew Skye to her and wrapped her arms around her in a tight hug. Skye rested her forehead on Ricca's shoulder.

Ricca closed her eyes and basked in the feeling of Skye in her arms.

This was what she had been missing her entire life.

She hadn't had a feeling like this ever.

Everything about holding Skye just felt whole.

This was her mate.

She would protect Skye and Rolf with her life. Rolf may be Skye's son, but her wolf already felt a connection with the little pup. Visions of him in wolf form came to her mind. Skye lifted her head and inhaled sharply.

Ricca trailed a finger along Skye's cheek and landed at her plump bottom lip. No longer able to resist, she leaned down and covered Skye's lips with hers.

Instant connection.

Ricca's wolf howled inside, confirming what she already knew.

Skye leaned into her and stood up on her toes. She wrapped her arm around Ricca's neck, locking them together.

Ricca growled, thrusting her tongue past Skye's parted lips. It was the only permission she needed. Her mate tasted of warmth and sunshine, and it was everything she would have imagined.

Skye's breathless moan sent a rush of arousal through Ricca.

The kiss grew deeper. The scent of Skye changed from her light flowery aroma to one of an intense, repressed sexual need.

Ricca spun Skye around, trapping her between the counter and her body. Their breasts brushed against each other. Ricca loved the feeling of Skye's soft body. She slid her hands up and threaded her fingers into Skye's dark tresses.

The first taste of her mate was something she would never forget. Lust rushed through Ricca's veins. Skye's supple lips were addictive, and it just opened the floodgates of passion. Ricca wanted more. She wanted to explore all there was to Skye, discover every mole, freckle, and scar she may have. She wanted to rip off her clothes so she could kiss and lick every inch of Skye's skin and then be rewarded with her first taste of what waited for her between Skye's thighs.

Skye's soft touch of her hand on the nape of Ricca's neck sent a shiver down her spine. A growl rumbled deep inside Ricca's chest.

Mate, her wolf snapped.

Her wolf demanded she claim Skye right now.

Ricca tore her lips from Skye's and blazed a hot trail of kisses along her jawline and buried her face in the crook of her neck. Her tongue skated along her supple skin.

It would only take one bite.

Her gums burned and stretched while her fangs descended.

No.

Not now. Not this way. She couldn't claim her

without speaking with her first. No wolf worth their fangs would ever claim someone against their wishes.

Ricca lifted her head and cupped Skye's face in her hands. Skye's darkened eyes were round and large.

Ricca could almost get lost in them.

A tremor snuck through Skye. Ricca tightened her hold on her. The scent of her arousal was so strong it almost brought Ricca to her knees.

"There is nothing wrong with you," Ricca whispered. She had to make Skye understand that no matter what had happened in her past, none of it was her fault. She loosened her hold on Skye's face and brushed her thumb along her skin. "My wolf and I like you very much."

Her gaze dropped down to Skye's swollen lips. The urge to taste them again was growing.

"I like you, too," Skye replied. She leaned into Ricca, brushing her breasts against hers. She rested her hands on Ricca's waist while a wistful smile spread across her lips. Her demeanor was playful, and Ricca liked this relaxed version of Skye. "I'm glad you were the enforcer chosen to protect me and Rolfie."

"I am, too." She reached up and tucked Skye's

hair behind her ear. She couldn't stop touching her mate. Her wolf prowled around, anxious to get to Skye.

Skye's stomach rumbled, breaking the silence. Skye gasped, a horrified look passing across her face.

Ricca grinned and couldn't help stealing another kiss.

This one was slow, deep and life-altering.

She had her mate in her hands.

CHAPTER FIVE

"Oh my, this was good." Skye sat her empty plate on the coffee table. She leaned back and patted her belly.

Ricca was pleased her mate was full and content from their simple dinner. Ensuring her mate was taken care of would be her life's purpose.

"We can go out tomorrow and get some things that you may want or need. They stocked the fridge and freezer with a few items. I'm sure there are specific foods or favorites you would want to pick up."

"I have been craving a Diet Coke." Skye

giggled. She faced Ricca on the couch and rested her head back on the cushion and focused her attention on her.

"Anything you need, we'll grab. I'll take you around town, too, so you can get to know it," Ricca offered.

"That sounds fun."

Ricca reached out and took Skye's hand in hers. She entwined their fingers together and pulled Skye to her. She slid across the couch next to Ricca.

Her beauty mesmerized Ricca. She was the luckiest wolf in the world. To stumble upon her mate who was beautiful and kind. There was so much she wanted to know about Skye.

"Tell me what happened," Ricca murmured. They would need to discuss what had happened between them in the kitchen, but first, she needed to hear what had Skye running.

Skye's body tensed, her hand constricting around Ricca's. She glanced down at their hands, blowing out a deep breath.

Ricca grew still, waiting for Skye to speak. She knew the basics, that something had happened back in her old town, and the pack there was planning to come after her and the baby.

Why? Ricca hadn't been told of the reason.

"Back home, I was a human who lived in a predominately wolf shifter town. My parents died years ago, and it was my brother and me. We were living a decent life. We didn't have much, but we had no complaints." Skye exhaled and tightened her hold on Ricca's fingers. "I began seeing Reade. I should have known better."

"What?" Ricca asked quietly.

"He was the alpha's son." Skye shrugged.

Ricca was confused on why that would make a difference. Humans and shifters entered into relationships all the time. This wasn't out of the norm.

"I was resistant at first, but Reade was very persistent. He was nice, caring, and a good guy, unlike his father."

Ricca wasn't sure she wanted to hear her mate talk about her prior relationship, but she wanted to know everything about this woman.

The good and the bad.

Pushing down the surge of jealousy, she focused back on Skye.

"Reade was stubborn and was determined to court me even though he knew I wasn't his true mate. His father did not like that and was furious he would lower himself to pursue a human. To

Barone, his son should just fuck me, use me as a play toy, but not mate with me."

Anger rippled through Ricca. This alpha was a royal asshole, and Ricca's wolf immediately hated him. She wanted to attack the wolf and tear his throat out.

A slight growl escaped Ricca. Skye's gaze flicked to hers, a small smile gracing her lips.

"I take it Reade was a rebel and didn't listen to his father." Ricca reached up and brushed the few strands of Skye's hair from her face.

"And that is how Rolfie got here." Her smile slowly disappeared. She exhaled and shook her head. "It's Rolf who Barone is after. There was a war between the humans and the shifters. One where I have lost so much."

Ricca remained silent, tightening her hold on Skye's hand. Her heart cracked from the sadness that radiated from Skye. Even though they weren't mated, she could pick up on Skye's emotions, and it was disturbing that such a beautiful woman could be haunted by something in her past.

"If you don't want to talk about it—"

"No, it's fine. I need to tell you what you are involved in." Skye sat up taller on the couch and blew out another shaky breath. "Barone took

Reade's death hard. He became even more vicious and demanded that I give my son to him. Rolf is his heir, and he wants my son. He can't have my baby."

Her words ended on a sob. Ricca gathered her close and held on to her while Skye's body trembled.

Her wolf snarled.

No one would take Rolfie from Skye.

She would fight to the death to ensure this woman was not separated from her child. Ricca lost track of time and wasn't sure how long they sat on the couch. She could stay there for an eternity if she needed to comfort Skye and make her feel safe.

"No one will take Rolfie away from you. This I promise you." Ricca brushed Skye's hair from her face again when she tilted her head back. Seeing the tears streaming down her skin gutted Ricca. They hadn't known each other long, but it didn't matter. Fate had placed Skye in Ricca's path to find her, and now that she had her, she refused to let anything stand in her way from claiming her. "We are going to do everything in our power to ensure you and Rolfie will have a good life here in Howling Valley. This is your new home."

"Thank you," Skye whispered. She reached up and wiped her cheeks. A nervous chuckle escaped her. "Are we going to discuss what happened in the kitchen?"

She turned her big brown eyes on Ricca who became lost her in her large orbs. Color was returning to her pale skin. Ricca could not lie to her mate. She would be honest. Right now wasn't the time to drop the bomb that they were mates after she'd just shared her past.

Ricca could be patient.

Her wolf, not so much, but she herself would wait for the best time to approach this subject.

"Do you regret it?" This was one thing she had to know. Her breath caught in her throat while she waited for Skye's reply.

"No." Skye shook her head. "Not at all. Just wondering if it will happen again."

Ricca's wolf threw her head back and howled. She paced immediately.

Mate, her beast snapped.

She clawed at Ricca's stomach, demanding to be let out.

No, calm down, she whispered to her animal. Her wolf snorted, and quieted, but she continued walking back and forth.

It was going to take a lot to settle her wolf. It was dark out, and she would need to check the perimeter, and she could do that in her wolf form to allow her to stretch her legs.

In due time, her animal would get the chance to meet Skye, but right now, she was going to have to wait. They needed to see to their mate first.

"It will, but not tonight. I want you to get some rest. Go shower and get some asleep. I'm going to go do a perimeter check."

They stood from the couch. Unable to resist, Ricca snagged Skye's hand and drew her close.

She leaned down and planted a soft kiss on Skye's lips. "I won't be long."

Skye spun around and walked into the master bedroom. She turned when she got to the door and glanced back to Ricca, shutting the door. Once she closed it, Ricca went outside. She inhaled sharply, not picking up any scents that shouldn't belong in the area.

She stripped her clothes off and left them on the top stair. Walking out onto the cool grass, she relaxed and permitted her animal to take over.

Ricca fell to the ground, allowing the change to overcome her. Her bones stretched and reshaped while dark fur burst forth through her skin. Within minutes her wolf was trotting off to the edge of the yard. She paused and looked back at the house.

The urge to return to Skye was strong, but Ricca pushed it down. Her animal's desire to meet Skye was evident.

Not now. Ricca sighed. *We need to make sure the area is safe for Ricca.*

That was all she had to say. She turned away from the cabin and went on the prowl to ensure there were no predators in the area that shouldn't be.

EXCITEMENT FILLED SKYE. She had thought with her having to be tucked away with an enforcer she would have to be hidden. Finding out the alpha endorsed her getting to know the town was a bonus.

She sat in the passenger seat of Ricca's SUV and basked in the feeling of the fresh air whipping in through the open window. Rolf was secured in his car seat in the back and was quiet, signaling he had dozed off.

Skye peeked at Ricca who was relaxed behind the wheel. Her silvery hair whipped around, and her eyes were obscured by her dark glasses.

Last night, Skye had the hardest time falling asleep. The shower had done her some good, but her body was still aroused. The kiss they'd shared had rocked Skye's world.

She'd never had that response before, and it left her baffled.

What did it mean?

There was no questioning the attraction between them. Skye had hoped Ricca would have come into her bedroom, but she hadn't.

"Did you make a list of everything you need?" Ricca broke the silence. She glanced over at Skye momentarily then focused on the road again.

"I did. There are just a few things I need, but I'm sure I'll think of something else once we are there." Skye bit her lip to keep from asking about what had happened in the kitchen. It had been on her mind constantly and had even invaded her dreams. All night she'd tossed and turned. Any other time she would have blamed it on the new environment, but that wasn't it. She had woken up sexually frustrated with the object of her desires sleeping out in the living room on the couch.

She held back a yawn and made a note to try to grab a nap with Rolfie later. Settling back, she took in the beautiful scenery that flew past.

"I don't know about you, but I need coffee. Want some?"

The woman must be psychic.

"Of course." She perked up at the mention of coffee. It was something she would admit she couldn't live without, and the last few days since getting on the road, it had been hard to find good coffee that wasn't tar in a cup.

"I know of a little bakery that is to die for. I still can't tell what my favorite item is. I've tried everything." Ricca grinned.

They arrived in town. Skye took in the picturesque brick buildings and well-manicured greenery. There were plenty of areas for pedestrians to walk and park benches scattered throughout. It was modern but yet still had an old-world charm to it.

The air was filled with the scent of flowers and nature with a slight hint of the ocean that wasn't too far away. Southern California appeared as if God himself had come down and painted the perfect area.

Skye breathed in and just felt welcome here in Howling Valley, and she had yet to meet any of the townspeople.

It was a just a feeling that overcame her as if she were meant to be here.

Off in the distance, a series of hills and mountains lining the backdrop of the town snagged her attention. Howling Valley was nestled between the rolling hills, tucked away in its own world.

"What's over there?" She pointed to the area.

"That's bear territory. The Brokenclaw Clan resides there." Ricca tipped her chin toward the mountains. "It's beautiful. I love to go hiking and camping up there."

"That sounds nice." Skye sighed and was making notes of all the areas she wanted to explore here. From the town to the hills, she was going to keep her and Rolf busy getting to know their new home.

A twinge of doubt entered her mind, reminding her of the danger that was following her.

She shook it away and was confident Evan and his wolves would be able to protect her and Rolf.

Ricca navigated her truck into a parking spot in front of a cute little bakery.

"We are here." Ricca killed the engine. She glanced at Skye with a grin. "You are going to love Echo's baking. That bear sure can bake."

Honey Bear Bakery.

CHAPTER SIX

Skye's stomach growled. She giggled and exited the vehicle. She slammed the door shut and moved to the back door and opened it. Rolf's wide eyes met hers. A silly grin was on his lips. He squealed and reached for her.

"So you are awake." She chuckled. She undid his safety belt and pulled him from his chair.

"Here, I'll grab his bag." Ricca reached around her, brushing against Skye's back.

Skye inhaled sharply at the feeling of Ricca touching her. The memories of last night raced forward. Her lips tingled as if she could still feel

Ricca's. She stepped back while Ricca took the bag and hefted it up on her shoulder. She closed the door and placed a hand on the small of Skye's back.

"Come. Let me feed you."

Skye tugged on her lip with her teeth and bit back a sigh. Her body automatically shifted closer to Ricca while they strode along the sidewalk toward the café. Ricca maintained her hand on Skye; the warmth of her touch sent a rush of emotions through Skye that she had never felt before.

Was this fate? She had been around shifters long enough to know they believed that everything happened for a reason and fate decided it all.

Hell, their mating was designed by an entity they couldn't see.

Fated mates were permanent. Once a shifter formed a bond with their other half of their soul, it was forever.

As a human, she had never really believed it in before.

But right now, she was thinking there had to be some truth to the notion.

Why else would she be reacting to Ricca the way she was? They had just met, and already she felt safe in her presence, trusted her with her and her son's lives, and felt a heightened attraction to this wolf shifter that she'd never experienced before.

She glanced at Ricca. As if sensing her gaze, Ricca's amber eyes fell to hers, and it was then Skye knew.

This was fate.

Maybe the reason she never believed before was because she hadn't met Ricca yet.

She had to admit, this felt right.

Her stomach grew into knots. How would she approach the subject with Ricca? Didn't wolves sense it first? Would her wolf accept Skye? Would Ricca reject her because she was human?

No.

What was she thinking? That kiss practically set the cabin on fire.

There was something between them.

And Skye wanted to explore it.

Ricca held the door open for her and motioned for her to enter. She stepped inside and was immediately accosted by the most delicious smells she'd ever breathed in.

"Oh my." Skye took in the café and immediately knew she was going to frequent this establishment. The scents of cinnamon and coffee beans grew stronger as she walked toward the counter.

The bakery couldn't be described by another way but cute. The decor was filled with warm rustic colors; the uncovered brick walls were painted white. Exposed dark-mahogany beams lined the ceiling that matched the tables. Chalkboards posted on the wall held the daily specials and menus.

There were a couple of women behind the counter working. A pretty brown-skinned woman was finishing up with the customer before them. There was a good number of patrons scattered around the establishment.

"Order whatever you want. We can even get some things to-go to take back to the cabin." Ricca stood next to her and waved at the woman behind the counter. "Hey, Echo."

"Ricca! How the heck are you?" A curvy woman with dark hair spun around from the machine she was tinkering on. Her apron was decorated with flour and what appeared to be chocolate. Her gaze landed on Skye and Rolf. "And who do we have here?"

Ricca quickly made the introductions. She didn't mention Skye and Rolf were on the run for their lives. Just that they were new to town and she was showing them around.

"You have a wonderful café." Skye offered the woman a smile.

"Thank you." Echo moved over to the register. "What can I get you?"

Skye was quite overwhelmed. She wanted to try everything, and it was hard to narrow it down. She finally made her decision and ordered.

"I promise we'll come back." Ricca ran her hand along Skye's back and moved close to her. "Echo has that effect on all of us. The woman puts something in her food that draws us back to her."

Ricca ordered her food, and Skye didn't hear one word. Her attention was focused on the sensation of Ricca's closeness and her hand skating along her back. The scent of her filled Skye's nostrils. She breathed it in, her body awakening slightly.

She wanted the wolf.

Ricca nudged her with her hip, breaking her from her thoughts. Skye blinked and turned to Ricca. Her grip on Rolf tightened.

"What did you say?" she asked.

"I said, go find us a table. I'll bring everything over." Ricca jerked her chin toward the seating area.

"Okay." Skye spun on her heel and headed toward the tables. Her face grew warm as she walked away thinking of all of the carnal things she wanted to do to Ricca. She glanced down at Rolf who reached up and tugged on her hair. "Come, little boy. Let's find a table."

She quickly found one with a half booth and chair. She took her seat on the booth and settled Rolf on her lap. The atmosphere of the place was welcoming, and all the patrons had the look of pleasure and bliss on their faces as they ate. Her stomach rumbled again, and she couldn't wait to dive into her food.

"Here we go." Ricca arrived at the table with a tray. She sat it down and hung Rolf's bag on the chair in front of their table.

"That smells so good." Skye groaned. She reached for her coffee and immediately took her first sip. A moan escaped her.

It was the best damn coffee she'd had in a long time.

Matter of fact, it might be in forever.

Ricca chuckled and placed her food in front of her. Skye had ordered steel-cut oatmeal with honey and fresh berries with a cheese Danish to quench her sweet tooth. She didn't want to imagine how many of the calories was going to go straight to her hips. She'd have to find time to work it off later.

"Are you going to be able to eat with little guy on your lap?" Ricca asked.

"Of course." Skye smiled down at Rolf. She glanced up at Ricca and tossed her a wink. "I've had plenty of practice."

Did she just wink at Ricca?

Where the hell did that come from? She couldn't remember if she'd ever done that before in her life.

"Okay." Ricca's eyes darkened. She took a sip of her coffee and tipped her cup to Skye. "If you need me to hold him, I can."

They ate their food in a comfortable silence. Skye was thankful her child was behaving. His wide eyes took in the restaurant. He quietly studied a few patrons sitting at the next table, leaning back against her.

"Have you always lived here?" Skye asked. She wanted to get to know Ricca. She wanted to know what made the enforcer tick.

"Yup. Born and raised here in Howling Valley."

"You said this was your first job? What did you do before you became an enforcer?"

Rolf reached for her spoon. She took a little oatmeal and placed it at his lips. He opened his mouth and allowed her to place a small amount inside. He chewed the oats and soon swallowed. He squealed, obviously enjoying the taste.

"I was actually in cyber security before I decided to apply to become an enforcer. My cousin, who I have always looked up to was one, and I sort of idolized him. I wanted to have a job where I felt like I belonged and that I could do something worthy and honorable."

"Well, I would say protecting a woman and child is definitely honorable," Skye murmured.

Their eyes met, and the sexual tension between the two of them thickened.

She prayed Ricca wouldn't have to place herself in danger just for her or Rolf. She wouldn't know what she would do if something happened to Ricca.

"Are you two enjoying your breakfast?" Echo breezed over to them. She took a seat in the chair across from them. Her warm eyes twinkled as her gaze landed on Rolf. She smiled and waved to him.

He laughed and raised his arms toward her.

"I am. It's so good."

"Can I hold him?" Echo asked. She was already halfway out of her seat and moving toward Skye.

"Sure." She laughed.

Rolf practically dove toward the woman. Echo lifted him and bounced him around.

"I just love the smell of babies." Echo sniffed the top of his dark curls and sighed. She reclaimed her chair and grinned at Rolf who was busy reaching for her hair.

"He smells good now. Should have been around this morning when he had a nice surprise waiting for me in his diaper." Skye took another healthy bite of her oatmeal. The flavors of the cinnamon and fruit burst out on her tongue. She sighed, wondering if she could recreate this at home.

"Oh, that's just being a baby." Echo giggled.

"He's a good baby. He's a charmer for sure. All the ladies are drawn to him," Ricca said.

Skye's heart warmed at how her son had been accepted by everyone so far. It wasn't because of who his father was or who his grandfather was, it was just him. He loved the attention.

Ricca was right. Women were drawn to him. She could already see he was going to be handful when he got older.

"Where did you get a baby from?" A toned woman with dark hair arrived at the table. She was dressed in jeans, a dark t-shirt, suspenders, and shit-kickers on her feet. Her eyes were that of a wolf, and heat practically consumed her gaze as she watched Echo with Rolf.

This had to be the bear shifter's mate.

"I just borrowed him, babe."

The newcomer snagged a chair from an empty table and brought it around next to Echo. She sat, and the two shared a quick kiss.

"Mindi, this is Rolf," Echo made the introductions. Her skin was flushed, and she had a wide grin on her lips. They made a beautiful couple. She motioned to Skye. "And this is his mother, Skye. They are new to Howling Valley."

"Hello." Mindi offered Skye a smile and turned her attention back to her mate. She rested her arm on the back of Echo's chair. She reached over and offered Rolf a finger. He promptly took it and tried to pull it to his mouth. "Hey, that's my finger."

Mindi took it back and chuckled.

"What's been going on with you, Mindi? I haven't seen you around lately." Ricca pushed her empty dish away and leaned back against the booth.

Skye hadn't noticed when they had gotten so close. Their thighs brushed each other. She inhaled sharply when Ricca's hand rested on her leg.

It was a slight touch, but possessive.

And Skye was loving it.

She glanced up and found Ricca watching her as if waiting for her to move it away.

"I've been extremely busy. With our recent shows, business has been booming." Mindi leaned over and nuzzled Echo's neck.

"Mindi is an amazing photographer. Her works always sell out when she has shows at her gallery. She's going to put Howling Valley on the map," Ricca said.

"Really? I would love to see your work someday." Skye loved good artwork. She didn't get a chance to indulge much back home. With the turmoil between humans and wolves, she wasn't able to enjoy the things she loved.

"Have Ricca bring you to the shop. I would love to snap a few photos of this little guy." Mindi nodded to Rolf who was trying to grab her suspenders.

Echo giggled and handed the baby over to her mate. They cooed and laughed at Rolf's antics.

Skye watched the two of them, and anyone could see they were in love. There was no denying the attraction they shared. Their light touches, kisses, and nuzzling gave Skye a warm feeling. She loved seeing two people who were in love with each other.

She turned and found Ricca's heated gaze on her. Skye's core clenched at the look. She tried her best not to get aroused because she knew any shifter within a close distance would be able to scent it.

Ricca's lips parted while her tongue snuck out and slid along her bottom lip. Skye's breath caught in her throat.

She would love to feel Ricca's tongue trail along her body. A tremor snuck through her at the thought of that same tongue parting her labia and diving in—

Stop!

Skye blinked. This was not the kind of thoughts she should be having while sitting around with Ricca's friends.

Once they were back at the cabin, she would allow the fantasy to continue, but she truly wanted the real thing.

IT HAD BEEN a while since Skye had been shopping with no worries. After they'd finished their breakfast and chatting with Mindi and Echo, they had strolled along the shops that were near the bakery.

It felt good to just pretend she wasn't on the run from her former pack.

The area of shops was one she would want to return to. There were other restaurants she wanted to visit, and wandering around gave her a sense of freedom she hadn't had in a while.

Now they were on their last stop at the grocery store. Ricca pushed the cart while she ambled along beside her carrying Rolf. He was getting fussy, and she knew it was nearing his nap time. His small hands kept pulling at her shirt, and that was his signal.

He was hungry.

"We're almost done." She kissed his forehead.

He blinked up at her, and his face scrunched up as a whimper escaped him.

Ricca paused and snuck an arm around Skye's waist and brought her close to her.

"What's wrong, little guy?" she asked.

The move was subtle, but it did things to Skye's libido. Skye didn't miss how well they fit together. She leaned into Ricca's embrace, resting her head on Ricca's shoulder briefly. She inhaled Ricca's scent and sighed. She didn't know what it was, but it was pleasing to her senses. She wanted to tuck her head in the crook of Ricca's neck and breathe it in more.

It felt good to be able to lean on someone.

"He's ready to be fed." She sighed. Her breasts tingled as if sensing they were in need.

A low growl emanated from Ricca's chest, and it appeared to calm Rolf down. She didn't know what it was, but it must be a wolf thing. He dropped his head down on her chest while Ricca ran a hand along his back.

Skye knew the feeling.

Ricca's touch did things to her, too.

"Let's hurry so we can take care of little man." Ricca released her, and Skye felt a slight disappointment.

They hurried along, but Rolf's whining was growing again.

Skye sighed and prepared for his all-out crying that was soon to follow. Rolf had a set of lungs on him that would rival a banshee. He was growing so much, and there were still things she was unsure of about raising a child, much less one who was part shifter.

She wished she had her mother to call on to ask questions, but sadly her parents weren't around. Sadness filled her that her family would never get to know her son. She was doing this mother thing solo and was learning as she went.

They finally arrived at the register where they were checked out swiftly. Ricca took care of everything and ushered them out of the store and to the car.

"I can help load the trunk," Skye offered.

"Nonsense. I've got this. Go take care of Rolfie."

Ricca kissed her lips, and Skye melted. She blinked and walked over to the truck and got in the back behind the driver's seat.

"Okay, sir." His whimpers were growing louder. She unbuttoned her shirt and opened her bra for him. Cradling him in her arms, she held him while he latched on to her. His little body relaxed against hers while he fed. His dark-brown eyes, so similar to his father's, watched her. "If only your father was here to see how big you've grown."

She brushed a dark curl from his face. Reade would have been a great father. She wasn't sure what would have been in the future for them, but she knew he would have been there every step of the way for Rolf.

The trunk slammed shut, breaking her from her thoughts.

Skye couldn't help but wonder. If Reade had still been alive and he'd come with her to Howling Valley, would she have met Ricca?

What would have happened if they did meet, and the chemistry was just as strong?

The laws of wolf mating would have ruled. He would have stepped aside so she could mate with—

"Everything okay back there?" Ricca slid into the driver's seat. Her voice was deep and husky. Their eyes met in the rearview mirror for a moment. Ricca broke their stare, her eyes straying down toward Skye's chest.

"Yes, he finally has what he wanted."

Now Skye had to put a plan in motion to go after what *she* wanted.

Ricca's eyes met hers again. Her eyebrows rose high, but she didn't say a word. The heat that flared to life in her amber eyes was a sign that the wolf shared similar thoughts.

Skye couldn't wait for the wolf to take what she was going to offer.

CHAPTER SEVEN

Ricca tightened her hands on the wheel. She breathed in the sweet scent of Skye's milk. Her ears picked up the sounds of Rolf greedily drinking his mother's nourishing substance.

Ricca had never been jealous of a baby before, and right now, she was downright green with envy.

What the hell is wrong with me?

She shook her head and tried to focus on the road. Now she should be giving Skye privacy while she fed her child, but she couldn't help it.

She snuck a peek in the rearview mirror, and her breath caught in her throat. Love and awe showed bright in Skye's face as she watched Rolf. Her hand slowly stroked his dark hair from his face. The creamy smooth skin of the swell of her breast made Ricca's mouth water.

What she wouldn't do to be able to see the entire mound. Her chest rose and fell swiftly while she tried to catch her breath. Her core clenched, and she was certainly glad humans didn't have advanced senses like shifters were born with.

If they had, there was no doubt Skye would smell the heavy scent of Ricca's desire for her.

The woman was downright beautiful. Her wolf whined, pushing against her chest. She wanted to claim Skye. The urge was growing stronger.

Could she?

Her wolf snapped.

Well, she knew what her wolf wanted.

Skye.

The human side of her did, too.

The shrill tone of her cell phone broke through the silence. Ricca glanced at the screen on her dashboard and saw Decker's name flashing. She pushed the hands-free button on her steering wheel to accept the incoming call.

"Hello?" she answered.

"Hey, Ricca," Decker's deep voice came through the vehicle's speakers.

"Decker." Ricca sat up straighter. From the tone of his voice, she knew this was a business call and not social one. Normally he was playful; they never used their formal names when addressing each other.

"The alpha is requesting you bring Miss Lennon tomorrow to the compound. He's set up a virtual meeting with the Blackmane's alpha."

Ricca's gaze met Skye's in the rearview mirror. The scent of Skye's fear was stifling.

Ricca's wolf's protectiveness overcame her. She fought to keep her fangs from descending. Her animal was ready to go to war for Skye.

They wouldn't allow anything to happen to Skye. She would ensure that Skye knew she would do everything in her power to protect her and her babe. She, nor her wolf, liked the fact that their woman was afraid of the Blackmane's alpha.

"Yes, sir. What time?" she asked. Her hands tightened on the wheel as she turned onto the dirt road that led to their cabin.

"Arrive around eleven in the morning. He wants to speak with her before the call."

"Not a problem."

"Everything going all right?" His voice softened slightly.

She bit back a smile. Her elder cousin was always looking out for her. He still saw her as a young pup, and she knew he would always have her back if she needed him.

"Yes. We grabbed breakfast at the Honey Bear Bakery then we went shopping to pick up a few things."

"Hmmm...Honey Bear Bakery. Good pick. Echo's food is world-renowned." He chuckled. Her cousin had a sweet tooth. He always appreciated when she brought him things from Echo's shop. "If you need anything, call me."

"Will do."

They disconnected the call. They arrived at the cabin a few minutes later. She parked the truck and killed the engine. She turned around to face Skye.

Her breath caught in her throat again at the sight of Skye's full breast. Her rosy-pink nipple was beaded and glistening. Ricca swallowed hard, unable to look away from it. Skye's hand came into view and lifted her bra back into place. Their eyes met, and Skye held her gaze as she re-covered her mound.

Her cheeks grew flushed while they stared at

each other. The fear that Ricca once scented was gone. Now in its place, the tangy aroma of Skye's arousal.

Ricca inhaled sharply, breathing it in.

Just the thought of Skye's pussy being slick now was enough to drive Ricca insane.

Rolf's impatient cry broke their moment.

They both jumped as he screeched and babbled.

"I guess he's ready to get out of the truck," Skye joked.

Ricca laughed and exited the vehicle and walked around the car to assist Skye out, but Skye was already standing by the truck with Rolf perched on her hip.

Unsure what to say, Ricca motioned to the stairs. The ambled along and sat on them. It was a bright and sunny day with the perfect temperature. The sounds of nature surrounded them in the woods.

"You don't have anything to be afraid of." Ricca turned and took a hold of Skye's hand. She had to touch her. The need to comfort her was over-whelming for Ricca. She'd never had this reaction to someone before. "You don't have anything to worry about."

"I believe you, but Barone is deranged, and he won't care about who he has to hurt to get Rolf." She gave Ricca's hand a squeeze then released her. She adjusted the baby sitting on her lap. She turned him around to where his back rested along her chest. The baby sat quiet, his eyes wide, taking in the beautiful nature surrounding them.

Ricca didn't blame the baby. It was an amazing sight to behold. That was why she loved Howling Valley. His little wolf would be pulled to the outdoors. It was in their nature to become one with the land around them. There was nothing better than shifting into her animal form and roaming through the woods and forest.

An image of her in her beast form running along a field with a smaller gray wolf came to mind. The tiny pup was not familiar to her. She had never seen it until now.

Was that Rolf?

Her animal grew excited thinking about teaching the young pup all he would need to now.

The aroma of Skye's fear returned.

"Reade tried to do as much as he could to protect us. Previous to Reade dying, Barone was more tolerable, only because Reade was there and would raise Rolf. His heirs were close to him, so he didn't focus on us as much. Now that Reade is gone, Barone became obsessed with keeping Rolf close to him." Her voice caught on a hitch.

Ricca remained silent. If she could, she would take all the fear away from Skye.

The only way she could do that was to ensure she remained safe.

Ricca tried not to think of the man who had fathered Rolf. Jealousy reared its head. This Reade fella was no longer amongst the living. There was nothing to be jealous about. She didn't want to think if Skye loved him.

Or of him touching her mate in an intimate way.

"My alpha will make sure you and Rolf are safe here. You will not have to worry about going back or having your baby taken away from you."

"You don't get it. No matter what Evan says to Barone, he's going to want a war. He's going to want to fight. He is unreasonable. He's dangerous, and no one should trust a thing he says." Skye reached up and wiped the wetness from her cheek.

Ricca wrapped an arm around Skye and pulled her toward her. She rested her face against Skye's hair. She breathed in Skye's flowery shampoo that she must have used. The need to touch her overtook Ricca.

"My brother died last year," Skye said. "Gabe was found dead, and no one could give me answers. I know Barone was involved somehow. My parents are gone, and now Gabe."

Ricca closed her eyes. If what Skye said was true, then it would make sense. If the alpha wanted to isolate her and make her depend on his son and his pack, then he would have to eliminate any foe. If Skye had wanted to leave, her brother would have been able to help her.

But look at her mate now.

No matter what was thrown in her path.

She still persevered.

Skye didn't realize how strong she was for leaving Half Moon Bay.

Anger filled Ricca at the thought that there wasn't anyone who had been able to help Skye.

"You did the right thing in leaving when you did."

"I did?" Skye lifted her head and glanced at her.

Ricca reached out and trailed a finger along her cheek.

"Yes, you did." Her wolf growled in agreement.

"Can I ask you a question?"

"Sure." Ricca's gaze dropped to Skye's plump lips. The urge to taste them was growing stronger, but now was not the time. She was here to comfort Skye, not to take advantage of her.

"I never know what to think when a wolf growls around me."

"My animal would never harm you," Ricca was quick to reply. Her wolf whined, wanting to be free so she could officially meet Skye and prove that she was safe around her.

"That's not what I meant." Skye blushed, a small smile playing on her lips. It was cute how she appeared to grow nervous. Her hands fussed with Rolf's clothes, straightening his shirt. "What does it mean when yours does it?"

"She's really protective of you and the baby," Ricca admitted without hesitation. It was the truth.

"Why?"

Ricca couldn't look away from Skye's large brown eyes. She was quickly drowning in them, and she never wanted to return.

"I made a vow to protect you, and me and my beast will honor that." It was the safest thing she could say at the moment. She didn't want to scare the woman away by blurting out she was her mate.

Her wolf huffed, wanting Ricca to tell Skye.

Her animal was hardheaded and strong-willed. She just wanted to forge ahead and demand Skye give herself to her.

The human side of Ricca wanted that, too, but knew Skye was already skittish being on the run for her and her son's life. Ricca made a promise to herself and her animal that she would approach the subject with Skye. She was a human and may not feel the call of the mating bond like shifters did.

"Thank you," Skye's breathless words broke the silence. She reached for Ricca and took her hand in hers.

Ricca's heart did a little pitter-patter. It was the first time Skye had acted on her own to touch her.

"I really appreciate everything you are doing for me. Today I was able to fully relax and enjoy myself and not have to look over my shoulder." Skye stood from the stairs and placed Rolf onto her hip.

Ricca pushed off the stairs and stood next to Skye. Her eyes connected with Rolf's, and again, she could feel his little wolf. It was curious, and she sensed it was playful. Pups normally didn't go through their first shift until around the age of five. She couldn't wait to be able to take him out and run along the hills with him.

Rolf mumbled incoherently, not taking his eyes

off her. Ricca tapped his chunky cheek with her finger. Her animal whined, and a low, soft growl escaped her.

"What's going on?" Skye whispered.

"Oh, nothing. My wolf can sense Rolf's. His animal will be a strong one when he's older."

"How can you tell?"

"He's connecting with mine. His wolf is seeking mine out." Ricca smiled. It was just another reason why she believed fate had meant for them to be together. Even the baby was supposed to be hers.

"That's wonderful. I was always concerned that since he was half human that maybe he wouldn't be able to shift or maybe not have a wolf." Skye's grin grew. The excitement in her was evident. She turned Rolf around to face her. She rubbed her nose against his. "Mommy's so happy there is a little wolf in you."

His giggles pierced the sky. He reached out and landed a slobbery wet kiss to Skye's face. Her laughter joined his.

The sight of the two of them happy and relaxed pleased Ricca. This was how Skye should always be. Whatever Ricca had to do to keep the fear away, she was willing to do it.

Instead of giving in to the urge to draw Skye to her and kiss, she motioned to the SUV.

"I'll grab the bags and take them in." Ricca didn't want for a response. She hightailed it to the truck to begin unloading it.

The squeals of the baby filled the air. A smile graced her lips. If only she could imagine this was a regular day and this was their home.

She glanced over at Skye smiling and twirling around in circles.

Determination surged through Ricca.

Skye and Rolf belonged to her, and she was going to make sure they both knew it.

CHAPTER EIGHT

Skye leaned against the doorjamb of her bedroom and waited to make sure Rolf was asleep. He had such a busy day. She'd fed him his first taste of veggies which he'd gobbled up and then she gave him a nice warm bath. After feeding from her, he was out like a light.

The little bugger was even snoring.

A smile ghosted her lips.

The way he'd taken to Ricca was nothing short of amazing. He loved getting attention from her. Skye didn't blame him one bit. Ricca was a gorgeous woman, and Skye could admit she'd love to be the center of Ricca's attention.

She reached for the door and pulled it closed, leaving it ajar just slightly so she would be able to hear Rolfie if he woke up. Turning around, she headed to the kitchen.

Ricca had cooked dinner, and Skye didn't want the shifter to think she couldn't carry her weight around the cabin. She didn't mind cleaning up the kitchen. Back home it gave her a chance to be able to think and get her thoughts together.

"Hey, I was going to do the dishes," Skye exclaimed. She drew to a halt in the middle of the small kitchen.

Ricca was already at the sink running the water. "Oh, it's not a bother. You were dealing with the baby." She glanced over her shoulder.

Skye flew to her side and playfully shoved Ricca away from the sink.

"You cooked. I clean." She grinned and tested out the water. It was warm, and the soap suds were growing taller. "I need to make myself feel useful while we are here."

"It's not a problem. You have the baby to deal with. Go and relax." Ricca bumped her with her hips. She took the plate out of Skye's hand and slid it into the water.

"I'm serious. I'll do the dishes." Skye grew bold and leaned into Ricca, brushing her arm with her breasts.

They paused, staring at each other. Skye didn't know what to think. She leaned closer to Ricca and wanted to kiss her again. Her gaze dropped down to Ricca's mouth.

The faint sound of Ricca's wolf growling cut through the tense moment.

Skye stepped back from Ricca. The sound of her beast was arousing for her. She liked the thought that Ricca's animal liked her. She wasn't afraid of Ricca.

"I'm sorry," Ricca whispered. She reached for Skye.

"What is she saying to you?" Skye understood that even though Ricca was in human form, her animal was trying to break through and communicate. It had to be the only reason why Ricca kept growling.

"Nothing." Ricca shook her head.

Skye didn't believe her. She stepped forward again, this time trapping Ricca against the sink.

Ricca's amber eyes glowed brightly. The growl sounded again, and Skye could no longer resist.

She stood frozen as Ricca lowered her head to hers. Skye's heart beat erratically. Ricca's soft, warm lips covered hers.

Immediately, Skye felt as if she were home. The scent of Ricca wrapped around her. The woman smelled of nature on a bright sunny day with a hint of the ocean.

Wrapped up in Ricca's arms, she felt safe.

Secure.

Skye relaxed into the kiss, opening her lips, granting Ricca's tongue permission to enter.

Ricca's arms tightened around her, holding her close. Their breasts strained against each other. Skye had the sudden urge to remove her clothing. She wanted to feel Ricca's bare body sliding along hers.

Ricca's hands pushed Skye away, breaking their kiss. She stared at Skye, darting past her. Skye turned and watched Ricca storm over to the back door. She flung it open and disappeared outside.

Skye stood stunned, unsure if she had done something to anger Ricca. Skye walked over to the door and glanced out into the darkness.

Ricca stood near the railing with her hands

resting on it. Her shoulders rose and fell in a rhythmic fashion.

"Ricca?" Skye stepped out onto the porch and paused. The cabin had an all-season porch attached to the back. It was furnished with a soft couch and chairs that would allow them to enjoy watching nature. There was a grill and a small picnic table for entertainment. Currently, the windows were removed to allow them to enjoy the fresh air. A gentle breeze blew as if signaled.

"You should go back inside." Ricca's voice broke the silence. Her head was bowed, and her long silvery hair hid her facial features.

"Did I do something wrong?" Skye took a step toward her. For some strange reason, she didn't want to leave Ricca alone. She had to be near her.

"No, you didn't." Ricca lifted her head and stared out into the darkness.

"We need to talk about that kiss." Skye sighed. She paused near Ricca and fought the urge to touch her. She watched Ricca, studying her features.

She didn't know what had spooked the wolf shifter.

"We shouldn't have done that. I shouldn't have touched you. It is not honorable."

"What's not honorable? The kisses we've

shared?" Skye grew shocked. She didn't understand Ricca's mindset.

"Just go back inside, Skye." Ricca turned to Skye, and it was then she was able to make out the tortured look on Ricca's face. The light shining from the open door highlighted her features.

"No. I won't. Talk with me. What is bothering you about the kisses? You have to feel the same attraction I do." Skye stepped closer and laid a hand on Ricca's arm. There was no way Ricca could deny the attraction. It had to be the only answer on why her wolf was always letting out growls.

The wolf was trying to communicate with her.

"I should have never touched you. I am to protect you. Keep you safe and—" She turned away and inhaled sharply.

Skye grew nervous as the silence drew out longer.

"Ricca."

"I will request in the morning for someone else to come and take over here." Ricca brushed past Skye and jogged down the stairs. She stopped in the middle of the yard and stood with her head tilted back.

Her words practically ripped Skye's heart out.

She rushed after Ricca and stopped behind her. The pounding of her heart filled her ears. She took in Ricca's tall, lithe form and felt the need to be near her.

Them separating was not what the fates would want.

Skye was sure of this.

"I don't want anyone else," Skye whispered. Without a doubt, Ricca's enhanced hearing heard her.

She grabbed Ricca by the arm and forced her to face her. She didn't want to lose Ricca.

She didn't know what this connection was that she felt with Ricca, but there was no way she was going to let her go without a fight.

"You are who I trust to keep me and Rolf safe. It's you who I need." Skye's voice broke. She moved closer to Ricca, closing the gap between then. She reached up and cupped Ricca's face.

Ricca's head swooped down, her lips taking Skye's in a hard, brutal kiss. Skye's heart skipped a beat. Ricca's tongue pushed past her lips, demanding entrance.

Skye wrapped her arms around Ricca's neck, holding her in place. She didn't want to risk Ricca having second thoughts. A groan escaped Ricca.

Her hands gathered Skye to her, skating down to hold Skye's ass.

Ricca tore her lips from Skye's and blazed a trail along her cheeks. Her hands slid underneath Skye's shirt and brought it over her head. The cool air caressed Skye's body, bringing goosebumps to her skin.

Skye returned the favor, removing Ricca's shirt. She went on a mission, wanting to get the wolf shifter naked. Skye's lips were drawn to Ricca's soft skin along her collarbone. She slipped her hands underneath the sports bra that covered Ricca's perky breasts. Once it was gone, Skye wasted no time capturing the first nipple with her mouth.

Ricca's moan and fingers threading into Skye's hair fueled her on. She loved the sound of Ricca's pleasure and wanted to hear it again.

Skye toyed with Ricca's nipple, suckling it deep inside her mouth. Her hands moved down to the edge of Ricca's pants. Within seconds she was pushing them and Ricca's panties down. Ricca kicked them off, leaving her naked.

"Your clothes. Off." Ricca's voice was husky and full of lust.

Skye's core clenched at the direct order. She glanced up and saw the burning heat in Ricca's eyes gazing down at her. She stepped back and chucked off the rest of her clothes. The wetness of her pussy coated her thighs.

Ricca reached for her, bringing her back, capturing her mouth again.

Their bare breasts brushed against each other. The hard beads of Ricca's nipples caressed Skye's. The warmth and feel of her skin increased Skye's arousal.

Skye knelt before Ricca. She pressed a hot kiss to Ricca's stomach.

A growl escaped Ricca.

Skye rested her forehead on Ricca's belly. She breathed in the musky scent of the woman she needed. Her heart's rapid rate leveled off, allowing her to inhale sharply. She relaxed her hands on Ricca's waist and looked up.

She was met by the amber gaze of Ricca. She spread her legs wide, granting Skye the permission she was hoping for.

Skye leaned forward and ran her tongue along the protruding bud that was waiting for her. Ricca's fingers were threaded into her hair. Her tight hold on the thick strands sent a shiver through Skye's body.

Out here in the open, she was getting her first

taste of Ricca.

There was nothing she would rather do than to have their first time be out in the open. The sounds of nature were the perfect backdrop to their lovemaking.

Skye licked Ricca's clit then suckled it. The tangy taste of Ricca exploded on her tongue. She leaned forward, licking as much of Ricca's cunt as she could before returning to her nub.

One glance up, and she took in Ricca standing with her head thrown back while she sucked on her clit. It was a magnificent sight to behold. Her breasts were thrust out, the shadow of her nipples evident.

Skye increased her pressure, and before she knew it, she found herself on her back with Ricca braced over her.

CLAIM HER.

Ricca's wolf demanded they take Skye.

She fought her animal. Now wasn't the time. Her fangs descended with the need to claim Skye.

The scent of Skye's arousal was consuming her. She inhaled sharply, a deep growl rippling through her. Ricca dragged her fangs along the column of Skye's neck.

She captured Skye's full breasts with her hands. The aroma of her milk greeted her. Her tongue slid along her beaded nipple. The faint taste of her sweet milk met Ricca. Her wolf rumbled, loving the taste of her nourishing essence. She suckled Skye's nipple inside her mouth. She teased and rolled the beaded nub with her tongue.

A moan slipped from her as she tasted more of the creamy goodness escaping the nipple. With a groan, she moved to the other breast and captured that one. Warm milk escaped it, and Ricca drank it all in.

Skye's small fingers gripped her hair, holding her in place. Skye's legs parted, allowing Ricca to settle into the valley of her thighs. She released the plump mound. Trails of her milky liquid slid along her tits.

Ricca licked both of Skye's breasts, not wanting to waste any of it. Skye's body writhed on the ground beneath her. Sexy gasps and moans escaped her, and Ricca's core clenched. She moved down, trailing her tongue along the soft belly until she maneuvered her way to Skye's creamy thighs.

"Ricca," Skye breathed.

The scent of her arousal was strong, and Ricca couldn't wait to dive in.

"Spread yourself open for me," Ricca murmured. She lay down on the thick grass, bringing her eye level with Skye's core.

Skye's thighs parted, revealing her slick folds.

Ricca's vision was excellent at night. She leaned forward and covered Skye's entire slit with her mouth. A groan escaped her the second she slid her tongue along her folds.

One taste of Skye's juices and she was addicted.

The tanginess exploded on her tongue. She dove in, pushing her tongue inside Skye. Her fingers gripped Skye's thighs while she lapped up all the creaminess escaping her core.

Skye's cries filled the air.

Ricca buried her face between her thighs. She feasted on her mate as if she was never going to get the chance again.

Ricca pushed two fingers inside Skye's core. Her slickness coated Ricca's fingers. Her tight channel contracted around Ricca. She captured Skye's clit with her lips, suckling and teasing her swollen nub.

Skye's hips rose to meet her. She slowly fucked Skye with her fingers while she continued to flick her clit with her tongue.

"Ricca!" Skye cried out. Her body arched off the ground while her body trembled.

Ricca reached up with her free hand and captured one of her breasts. She squeezed it while she continued to focus on Skye's pussy.

Her breast was covered in wetness from her milk that was escaping. Ricca's finger played with her nipples and massaged it. Skye's hand covered her hand to hold it against her.

Pushing her other fingers deep inside her, Ricca held them in place while she increased the pressure on Skye's clit. She tugged on the swollen flesh and curved her fingers, hitting a certain spot inside her lover.

Skye's body stiffened just as a scream escaped her. A warm gush of liquid rushed from her core, covering Ricca's hand and mouth.

Skye's body relaxed on the ground. Ricca withdrew her fingers and licked them clean of Skye's release. Skye's chest rose and fell swiftly. Ricca kissed along her mate's thigh.

Satisfaction filled her. She and her animal were pleased that they were able to elicit such a response.

She dropped a soft kiss to Skye's labia.

This was her woman.

This was her pussy, and she wanted more of it.

CHAPTER NINE

Ricca opened her eyes and glanced down at Skye nestled in her arms. They had finally managed to move from the yard to the couch on the back porch.

There was nothing that could make this night better. As much as she tried to resist, Skye would not let her avoid what was between them.

Her wolf paced inside her at the memory of Skye coming for her. She was pleased Skye felt the attraction between them.

It had to be nothing but fate.

She pulled Skye back against her and nuzzled

her face into the crook of Skye's neck. Her naked body was soft and warm.

A shiver passed through Skye.

"Are you cold?" Ricca asked. She moved her body closer to Skye. The couch was small, and they were spooned together.

"No. You wolves' bodies always run hot. I wish I did." Skye turned over and faced Ricca. She slid closer, closing the gap between them, resting her head on the curve of Ricca's neck.

Ricca pushed the hint of jealousy from her mind. Just thinking of Skye's former lover and father to Rolf had her wanting to attack someone. She didn't want to think of Skye cuddling with the other wolf, or spending time with him, or him making her smile.

Ricca's wolf growled, ready to attack the other wolf.

But Reade was dead.

He was the man who'd gifted Skye her child she loved so much.

She didn't want to think of him touching and tasting her mate.

Skye belonged to her.

Claim her.

Her animal was not taking no for an answer.

Now is not the time, she snapped back.

Her animal paced, brandishing her fangs. There were times she would have to battle her animal, and now was one of them. Lucky enough, the human side of her was stronger than the beast.

She was the dominant of the two, and her animal was going to have to trust her.

Soon, she promised.

Her animal snapped again and flopped down, unhappy.

Ricca placed a kiss to Skye's forehead. She was going to have to speak with the alpha. She didn't know what she was going to say but admit that Skye was her mate.

Her alpha was a fair one. He would never challenge fate. She would go to him and have a conversation with him. Once she explained that Skye belonged to her, there shouldn't be a problem.

Now that she had gotten a taste of her mate, she was thinking more clearly.

"What are you thinking about so seriously?"

Ricca looked down and found Skye staring at her with curiosity burning bright in her eyes.

Ricca smiled and dropped a kiss on Skye's lips.

"Just the conversation I need to have with the alpha."

"Oh?" Skye's eyebrows rose.

"Yes, but nothing for you to worry about," Ricca promised. She slid a hand along Skye's spine. She stopped at the swell of her ass. She trailed her fingers along the curve of her bottom.

"Will this talk have something to do with us?" Skye asked.

Ricca smiled again and lowered her head. She captured Skye's lips with hers. Her mate was too smart for her own good.

Their kiss was slow and deep. Skye's lips opened, her tongue welcoming Ricca's inside her mouth. Their tongues dueled together in a rhythmic dance.

Ricca shifted her body to cover her mate's. Skye's legs parted, allowing her to settle between them.

"Don't think kissing me will distract me from you answering." Skye giggled.

"I'm not sure what you're talking about." Ricca grinned and cupped Skye's breast. She gently licked around Skye's mound, ending at her nipple. She closed her lips around the bud and flicked it with her tongue. A pebble of milk appeared on it.

Ricca savored the taste of Skye's milk. She drew more of it inside her mouth, swallowing it. Skye arched her back, allowing her breasts to be pushed farther toward Ricca.

"I'm thinking you and Rolf will be competing for my breasts." Skye laughed breathlessly. She brushed Ricca's hair from her face while caressing Ricca's cheeks.

The sweet nectar flowed into Ricca's mouth. She continued drinking it, unashamed of the need for her to consume it. Ricca had always had a sweet tooth, and Skye's breast milk was sweet as honey.

"Maybe." Ricca released Skye and licked up the trickle of milk sliding along her breast. "It would be the perfect lesson to learn sharing."

Skye fell into a fit of giggles. Ricca kissed both of Skye's breasts, loving the sound of her mate's laughter.

Ricca lifted her head, a sound in the woods capturing her attention. She stared over across the yard and didn't see anything.

"What's wrong?" Skye asked.

"I need to go patrol," Ricca replied. She glanced down at Skye's naked body and didn't want to leave her. Her supple form demanded Ricca's attention, but for now, she had to go do her job and ensure they remained safe.

The need to protect Skye was strong.

Her beast was ready to come forward.

"Okay." Skye guided Ricca's face down to hers. She pressed a soft kiss to her lips. "When you come back, we can go to bed. Together."

Ricca's heart leaped. Her emotions swirled around inside her. Sharing a bed with her mate was a dream come true. She had never thought she would get to find the one who was meant for her.

There was no way they weren't going to share a bed together. Once she got the blessing from her alpha, they were going to share more than a bed.

They'd begin sharing their entire lives together.

"Go inside. I'm going to shift and check a few things out." Ricca pushed off the couch and stood.

"I want to meet your wolf." Skye sat up and swung her legs around and rested her feet on the floor. She stood beside Ricca and took her hand in hers. "I want to see what you look like."

Ricca raised their joined hands and kissed the back of Skye's.

"A quick meeting and then you go inside." Ricca released Skye and walked down the stairs. The cool grass met her bare feet. She turned around and found Skye standing on the stairs.

Ricca grew jealous of the moonlight that caressed Skye's naked, full breasts and wide hips.

Her body should never be covered and hidden away.

Ricca spun around and allowed her beast to come forward. Her fangs descended while she fell forward on the ground. Her bones lengthened and reshaped while fur burst forth through her skin. Once the transformation was completed, Ricca saw Skye standing at the bottom of the stairs.

Her animal was excited to finally be free in the presence of their mate. Ricca stepped toward Skye. Her animal grinned and stopped in front of Skye.

"Look at you," Skye murmured. She reached out and ran her hand through the fur on the top of Ricca's head. Her animal pushed forward, pressing her head to Skye's stomach. "Such a beauty."

Ricca's animal was pleased that Skye thought she was beautiful. She took a few steps away from Skye. Turning around, she raced off into the woods.

The sounds and scents of the outdoors were much more enhanced while she was in her animal form. The beasts wanted to race off and go hunting, but they didn't have time for such shenanigans.

We are working, she reminded her animal.

She slowed down and forged through the area. She took in the scents around her, not finding anything out of the ordinary. She didn't know what had caused the sound earlier. A few scents of deer and small game were picked up as she made her way through the thick forest.

It had to be one of them that had created the sounds. She continued on along the property and paused when she came across a scent she didn't recognize.

Who the hell is this?

Ricca's animal tensed. She roamed the area, memorizing the scent of the unknown wolf. If she were to smell it again, she would recognize it. She continued along and discovered that whoever it was had stayed in this area.

She paused and lifted her head and took in the front of the cabin.

Whoever had been there had stood and watched the house.

Ricca growled.

Her animal was on full alert now.

Whoever it was better keep their distance. She was a wolf who was protecting her mate and she wouldn't hesitate to attack.

She would have to notify the alpha of the unidentifiable smell. Even if he would have sent someone to check in on her, she would have recognized the enforcers' scents.

Ricca finished her patrol and headed toward the house. She padded toward the back. She shifted to her human form then went up the stairs. She paused in front of the door and glanced over her shoulder. She didn't see anything moving around.

Going inside the cabin, she closed the door and flicked the lock. She made sure all of the windows were closed as well. She walked around the house and ensured the front door was secured. It was getting late, and they were due at the alpha's house in the morning. She didn't want to alert anyone at this time.

She had done as she was trained to do. Check out the area, assure there was no danger, and stay close to the target.

If she called Decker now, he would ask her if she had done all of those things. This may be her first assignment, but she didn't want to appear as if she couldn't handle it. The alpha had faith in her to give this to her. She would prove to him that she had been the best person for this job.

She stood still in the living room and closed her eyes, utilizing her shifter's abilities.

There was no threat around them. Finally, she relaxed. She opened her eyes and found Skye standing in the doorway to the bedroom.

"Everything all right?" Skye asked. She had covered herself with a thin cotton robe. Her pebbled nipples pushed against the material, drawing attention to them.

Ricca made her way to her mate. Her breath caught in her throat at the sheer sight of Skye's beauty.

"Yeah. Nothing to worry about." Ricca didn't want to worry Skye. She reached out and ran a hand along Skye's arm. Her protective nature was still present. This woman before her meant the world to her.

This was the reason why she existed.

To protect and love Skye.

"I was about to take a shower. I feel like I smell like the outdoors." Skye laughed.

Ricca leaned in and inhaled briefly. She reached up and pushed Skye's dark hair away from her face.

"You smell good to me," Ricca said. She didn't know what Skye was complaining about, but the only thing she could scent was Skye and herself.

Her wolf stood to attention at the smell of herself on Skye.

"You're just saying that. Come. Join me." Skye didn't wait for an answer and took Ricca's hand in hers. She led them to the bathroom.

Ricca glanced over at Rolf's little bed and found him on his stomach still sleeping. Her wolf whined, the need to protect the baby just as strong as it was for Skye. Her animal wanted to meet the baby, too.

In due time, Ricca assured her.

Once in the bathroom, Skye walked over to the shower and switched the water on. She stepped back and turned to Ricca. The robe dropped from her and slid to the floor.

"You're so beautiful," Ricca murmured.

"You are, too," Skye replied. Her warm brown eyes grew larger. She marched over to Ricca and stopped in front of her. She took Ricca's hand in hers. "I've thought of nothing but you since we first met. I knew I wanted you."

Ricca's heart stuttered. She had never had someone be so forthcoming to her. Ricca had always believed that fate would send her the one person meant for her, but never would she have believed that she would be so lucky to have a beautiful woman who she could claim.

"I haven't been able to stop wanting you from the moment we met," Ricca admitted. She reached up and brushed Skye's hair away from her face.

"Then why did you say you would have someone else come and protect us?"

"Because I panicked. I've never had these feelings before and I don't want to——" She paused, not wanting to ruin the moment.

"Don't want to what?" Skye closed the gap between them.

Ricca gathered Skye to her and kissed her forehead. The feeling of her woman pressed close to her was enthralling. Her body was responding to Skye's nakedness. Her smooth, soft skin was arousing Ricca. The memory of Skye's pussy came to mind.

She wanted it again.

"I don't want to ruin my chance with you." She cupped Skye's cheeks and kissed her lips.

"I'm all yours."

Those three words caused the desire for Skye to explode within Ricca.

Her hand shot out and gripped Skye's face while she slammed her lips onto hers. She lost all control.

Skye wrapped her arms around Ricca's neck. Her lips opened, allowing Ricca's tongue to sweep inside.

Ricca reached down and lifted Skye into her arms. Her legs wrapped around Ricca's waist. She carried her into the shower. The warm water flowed around them.

Ricca tilted her head, deepening the kiss. She propped Skye against the wall while she continued to plunder her mouth. She captured all of Skye's moans and gasps. She slid a hand between them, her fingers finding their way to Skye's core. She parted her labia and exposed her clit.

Ricca wasted no time in stroking the little bundle of nerves.

"Yes," Skye cried out, tearing her lips from Ricca. She tilted her head back, offering her neck to Ricca.

A growl escaped Ricca. The sight of Skye's neck being presented had her fangs descending.

Her gaze zeroed in on the soft flesh. The desire to sink her teeth into her woman's neck and claim her was growing strong.

She didn't know how much longer she was going to be able to resist. They hadn't had the conversation of mating.

Claiming someone without their permission was a punishable offense.

Ricca lowered Skye to the floor, allowing one of her feet to touch down. She held Skye's other leg up in the air so she could continue to strum her clit.

Ricca nuzzled her face into the crook of Skye's neck.

"I want you," she murmured. She nipped Skye's skin gently. She slipped her fingers through Skye's slit, finding it drenched. She sank two fingers deep inside Skye.

"You can have me."

"All of you."

"Yes," Skye whimpered.

Ricca thrust her fingers inside Skye harder. She braced Skye's leg on her forearm to open Skye fully to her.

"Mine."

"Yours."

Ricca needed to consume all of Skye. The intense need to taste every part of her was over-whelming.

Using her thumb, she applied pressure to Skye's clit while she continued to sink her fingers into her.

"Ricca." Skye's breathless moan was driving her insane.

Ricca curved her fingers around and continued her motions. Skye's hands rested on her shoulders while she held on. Her head was tilted back against the wall, while her eyes were closed.

"Look at me," Ricca demanded. She wanted to

make damn sure Skye knew who was giving her pleasure. The jealous beast inside her wanted to make sure there were no thoughts of Reade in Skye's mind.

Skye's beautiful brown orbs locked in on her. Ricca withdrew her fingers and rubbed Skye's clit faster. Her fingers were slick with Skye's juice, gliding along her swollen flesh.

She watched Skye's emotions flutter across her face. She leaned down and captured Skye's lips just as her body grew tense.

Her nails sank into Ricca's shoulders while her orgasm rushed through her small body. She trembled with the force of her release. Ricca ignored the pain from her nails digging into her skin. Any marks would be gone within hours from her shifter healing ability.

Ricca gathered Skye to her. The kiss turned tender and slow. Skye's arms snaked their way around Ricca's waist.

Ricca's wolf settled down. She was happy they were with their mate, but soon, she was going to demand again that they claim Skye.

CHAPTER TEN

Rolf's whining grew louder. Skye exhaled, no longer able to ignore him. She gazed over at Ricca and found her still asleep. Not wanting to wake her, Skye rolled out of bed and made her way over to her son. He had pushed himself over onto his back.

He instantly ceased whining when he saw her.

"Hey, buddy. What are you fussing for?" she whispered. She reached down and picked him up. She was still naked, having slept that way next to Ricca. She loved the feeling of the wolf shifter lying next to her in the bed. Their bodies had been entwined all night, and it was comforting to Skye. It had been a long time since she had shared a bed with someone.

When Reade was alive, she had liked lying next to him, but there was something different between him and Ricca. With Reade, he made her feel safe and it was just nice.

With Ricca, it was a pure need to be next to her. Even standing a few feet away from her had her feeling sad.

"Let's get your butt changed, then I'll feed you." She kissed the top of his dark curly hair. Her breasts were feeling heavy, signaling it was time for her to express. She bit back a giggle. She now had two people who liked suckling her breasts.

But her child would always get first dibs on her milk.

She looked over at Ricca who was lying on her back. The sheet had fallen away from her, putting her high, full breasts on display.

Skye grabbed what she needed to change her little man. She laid him on the bed and quickly made short work of getting him in a new dry diaper. She tossed the soaked one in the trash in the corner.

He gave her his goofy grin and reached out for

her. She scooped him up and lifted him into her arms.

"Come on, silly boy." She walked over to the bed and slid back onto the mattress. He was already trying to get to her breast. She settled back against her pillows and cradled him in her arm. He settled down once he latched on to her breast.

The bed beside her shifted. Skye glanced over to find Ricca staring at her.

"Morning," Skye whispered.

"Morning." Ricca pushed up and settled back against the headboard. She brushed her long silvery hair from her face. Her gaze settled on Rolf. "Is there anything I can do for you?"

"Nope. We're good. He now has a dry diaper and his food." She chuckled. Her little greedy son was pulling hard on her. He must have been hungry. He had done so well and slept all night. The sunlight was flowing into the windows. She didn't know what time it was, but it was apparently time for Rolf Westway to eat.

They were due at the alpha's house, and she picked up that Ricca was nervous or something. It didn't take a rocket scientist to conclude Ricca was nervous about sharing their relationship with the alpha.

Skye knew the opinion of Ricca's alpha was important to her.

Ricca moved over and brought Skye to her. Skye rested back against Ricca while her arms came around to support her.

"You're a good mother," Ricca murmured. Her warm breath brushed Skye's ear. She glimpsed over at her and smiled.

"Thank you." Skye turned her attention back to her son. His eyes were closed as he continued to feed from her. She brushed his hair from her forehead. "He's my entire world."

"I know."

Something in Ricca's voice caused Skye to look over at her. There was a strange expression in her eyes. Their amber color was brighter as she gazed down at Rolf. It wasn't threatening but comforting. Her wolf would protect her son.

Skye only hoped Ricca wouldn't have to.

She exhaled and prayed the meeting with her father-in-law would go well, but it was a silly wish. Barone was not going to give up on getting his grandson back.

Rolf was his heir.

"It's going to be all right," Ricca said. She tightened her hold on Skye.

"How did you know what I was thinking?"

"You tensed up suddenly." Ricca brushed a soft kiss to her shoulder. Her hand came around and rested on Skye's.

They threaded their fingers together. Just having Ricca next to her was comforting.

Ricca dropped another kiss on Skye's bare shoulder. "But have no fear, my darling. You and Rolf won't have anything to worry about. We will get this all straightened out. Howling Valley is your new home."

"With you?" Skye grew bold with her question. Her mind was already made up.

She belonged with Ricca.

Ricca placed another kiss on her shoulder but didn't answer her. It made Skye even more determined to go after what she wanted.

She switched Rolf to the other side and allowed him to continue feeding. It was relaxing having Ricca next to her to share in this time. Skye leaned back with her eyes closed while the gentle tugging of Rolf on her breast soothed her.

Soon the motion on her stopped.

She glanced down at Rolf and found him fast asleep. His mouth was slightly open, and trails of milk ran down his cheeks. She wiped his mouth off with her fingers. She lifted him and rested his head on her shoulder.

"Do you want me to put him in the bed?" Ricca asked.

"No, I got him. I don't want to risk waking him." Skye scooted to the edge of the bed and stood. She moved over to the pack-and-play and placed Rolf down onto his bed.

She stood upright and faced Ricca. Skye stood at the foot of the bed and was frozen in place. Ricca's amber eyes were locked on her. She kicked the blanket off her and waved Skye forward.

"Come here, Skye." Ricca's husky voice had that low, commanding tone.

Skye knelt on the edge of the bed and crawled up toward Ricca who was propped up on the pillows. Her legs were spread open, showcasing her center.

Skye's gaze dropped down to her pussy. She licked her lips, wanting to get another taste of Ricca.

Skye stopped and bent down, lying across the bed. She pressed her hands to Ricca's thighs to hold them part. She leaned forward and ran her tongue along Ricca's seam.

"Yes," Ricca hissed. Her hand slid down to her lips and spread them open, revealing her clit.

Skye didn't waste any time in suckling the tiny bud.

"Make me come," Ricca said.

Skye trembled with the need to fulfill her wolf's command.

Her tongue traveled along Ricca's slick pussy, gathering all of the delicious juices. She was going to ensure her wolf would get exactly what she wanted.

Her tongue brushed along Ricca's clit again, eliciting a cry from her lips.

"Don't wake the baby." Skye chuckled. She kissed Ricca's inner thigh before returning to her activities.

She sank a finger inside Ricca. She made a deep sound, her hips thrusting forward. Skye introduced another finger inside her, stretching Ricca's channel. She was fascinated watching her fingers disappear into Ricca. The smooth channel contracted around her fingers. The sounds coming from Ricca were incoherent. They were a mix of growls and gasps.

Skye closed her mouth around Ricca's clit and suckled and licked it. Ricca's juices flowed out of her and coated Skye's hand and mouth. She continued on, wanting to push Ricca to her limit.

Her body stiffened as her climax hit her. She snatched a pillow from the bed and covered her own face. Her muffled cry was music to Skye's ears. She grinned and withdrew her fingers from Ricca's tight core. She swiped her tongue along Ricca's slit one last time and crawled up over her wolf.

Ricca tossed the pillow to the side and grabbed Skye by the back of her neck and brought her down on top of her. Ricca kissed her hard—this time, there was no doubt in what she was feeling. She rolled them over until she was braced over Skye. Their legs became entangled together.

Their soft moans filled the air while they writhed against one another. Ricca spread Skye's legs and straddled her. Their slick pussies slid along each other.

Skye gasped, biting back a cry. She had to try to remember that her child was asleep in his bed.

But the feeling of Ricca's pussy against hers was a dream come true. This was one of the most intimate positions they could be in, and she loved every second of it.

Ricca was not gentle in her possession of Skye.

She thrust her hips hard, gliding her clit against Skye's.

She leaned down and gripped Skye's hair, holding her in place. Her warm body covered Skye's completely. Her strong, lithe frame fit perfectly over Skye's soft curves.

She loved the feeling of Ricca taking control of their lovemaking. Her toned body strained against Skye's. Their breasts were crushed between them. Ricca's thrusts were hard and fast. Skye spread her legs wider and held on to Ricca's hips. The wetness from their arousal spread over them, allowing them to glide together in harmony.

Skye thrust her hips up to meet Ricca's. She whimpered, her nails digging into Ricca's hips.

There was a pulse of energy surrounding them. Skye wasn't sure what it was, but she knew it had to do with her wolf. Ricca tugged on her hair, turning her face away from her, exposing her neck.

Skye's heart pounded away.

Was this the moment Ricca would make her hers?

She closed her eyes, waiting for the pain of the wolf's bite, but it never came. Ricca bathed her neck with her tongue, dragging her fangs along her skin.

Skye would admit she was slightly disappointed Ricca didn't claim her. She wanted to feel the piercing bite of her lover.

Didn't wolves take their mates when they wanted?

Their movements grew frantic as they rubbed their sensitive buds together. Skye shuddered, her climax drawing near.

Ricca released the hold on her hair. Skye took advantage and faced Ricca who immediately claimed her lips. Their bodies grew tense at the same time, just as the power of their orgasms overtook them.

Together, their rode the waves of the most intense climax Skye had ever had. Her scream was captured by Ricca's mouth. Her arms wrapped around Ricca, gripping on for dear life.

The pleasure was too intense. She clenched her eyes shut, but tears still seeped out. Ricca ground her hips to Skye's while she continued to come.

Ricca fell onto Skye. Her weight wasn't crushing at all. She liked the feel of Ricca's solid weight on top of her.

They lay together for what seemed like hours. Skye didn't have one complaint. If sex with Ricca was always like this, she was ready to sign up for the next crazed lovemaking session.

Ricca rolled off of Skye and brought her into her side. She leaned over and nuzzled Skye's neck.

"Silent sex has to be the best sex out there," Ricca murmured. Skye covered her mouth to keep from laughing out loud.

"You've never had to stay silent before?"

"No." Ricca pulled the blankets over them and tucked them in. She moved in the bed and wrapped her body protectively around Skye's. "We're going to have to do that again so I can test it out."

"Anytime, love." Skye smiled and settled back into Ricca's embrace. She was sated and warm with her lover's arms around her. She allowed sleep to take her.

CHAPTER ELEVEN

Ricca guided the SUV onto the road that led to the alpha's home.

She was nervous.

Before they'd left the cabin, she should have brought up what was bothering her. She wasn't sure how Skye was going to react when she admitted they were mates.

How would Skye take the news?

As a human, would she understand the magnitude of mating?

Ricca glanced over at Skye who was sitting in the passenger seat with a small smile on her lips.

Skye had been in a pleasant mood since they had woken. They had shared a beautiful morning together and cooked a delicious meal then prepared to leave for the trip to the alpha's home.

"What are you smiling about?" Ricca asked.

"I'm just trying to keep a positive attitude about this meeting." Skye's demeanor changed immediately.

Ricca hated that she had asked. This was a stressful time for Skye. This confrontation with her father-in-law had to go well.

Ricca was confident Evan would be able to handle everything. He was a powerful man, and their pack was a strong one, too.

The other alpha would have met his match in Evan.

"That's what you have to do. We can't be defeated before we even arrive to the fight." Ricca reached over and took Skye's hand and gave her a squeeze.

"Thanks." Skye returned the gesture and held on to Ricca's hand. "I don't know what I did to deserve someone like you, but I am thankful."

"It's fate," Ricca replied without thinking. Her gaze cut to Skye who was already staring at her.

Shit.

"Fate?" Skye's eyebrows rose sharply. "As in, we were meant to be?"

Ricca tightened her grip on the steering wheel. There was no time like the present to approach the subject. The other wolves were going to scent Ricca on Skye. Even with a shower, their ability to pick up scents were heightened due to their shifter nature.

They arrived at the alpha's home. She parked the vehicle in front of the house and killed the engine.

"What if I said it was true?" Ricca asked softly. She caught sight of Decker coming out of the alpha's front door. They were running out of time.

Skye's eyes grew round as she stared at Ricca.

Decker jogged down the stairs and made his way to the truck.

"I'd say that it would explain a lot."

Ricca froze in place, unable to turn away from Skye.

A tapping at the window drew her attention. Decker was standing by the truck. He leaned down so he could look into the window. She conjured up a smile and opened her door slightly. He moved to allow it to open all the way.

She wished they had another minute or two, but they had to get inside. The alpha was going to want to speak with Skye prior to connecting with the other alpha.

"Everything good?" he asked.

"Yeah, we were just chatting." She hoped he didn't ask what their conversation was, because at the moment, she was too shocked to come up with a lie.

"The alpha is wanting to speak with Skye." He tipped his head to Skye who had stepped from the truck and was already opening the back door to get Rolf out.

"I know. We're not late." Ricca glanced down at her watch. She had made sure they'd left early enough to give them plenty of time to arrive.

"I'm ready." Skye slammed the door and hefted Rolf up on her hip.

There was so much they had to talk about, but that was going to have to wait.

Was Skye truly aware what it meant to be fated mates?

Ricca followed her cousin and Skye into the home. They were led to the alpha's office where he was sitting behind his desk.

"Ms. Lennon, it is good to see you." Evan stood from his chair.

"Likewise." Skye nodded, a small smile reappearing on her lips.

Rolf greeted the alpha with a squeal. His laughter was infectious, and they all chuckled. The baby waved at the alpha playfully.

"Please, have a seat." He waved Skye to the chair in front of his desk.

She walked past him, and he froze. The alpha flicked his gaze to Ricca, and it was at the moment she knew he had picked up her scent on Skye.

"I take it Ricca is treating you well?" the alpha asked.

Ricca stood straighter. Her animal was appalled the alpha would ask such a thing. Of course she would be taking care of her mate.

Calm down, she murmured. Her animal paced back and forth, unsettled. The last thing she needed was for her animal to try to challenge the alpha.

As if sensing her animal's irritation, the alpha glared at her. She immediately lowered her eyes to the floor. Of course, he *would* pick up on her animal's behavior.

She moved with Decker into the room and stood off to the side by the door. Her cousin gave her a curious look, but he didn't say a thing. She knew she was going to have to offer up an explanation later when they were alone.

"We are going to meet with Barone via video chat. He was resistant to the notion and had a few choice words for my assistant," the alpha began. He sat on the edge of his desk and folded his arms in front of him.

"I'm sure I can imagine what he said." Skye sighed. "Anything along the lines of tell that bitch to give me my heir?"

Ricca stiffened.

"Almost word for word." The alpha's low chuckle rumbled through his chest. "But don't worry. We won't be handing anyone over to him."

Skye held Rolf close to her chest. Her body posture was stiff, and her voice was devoid of all emotion. Ricca didn't like this side of her mate. She wanted to go to her and wrap her arms around her to comfort her, promise her that no harm would come to her and her child.

"Thank you."

Had it not been for her shifter hearing, Ricca may have almost missed her low words. Ricca clenched her hands together so tight she had to relax them, for her claws had burst through. She glanced down, expecting to see blood dripping from her palms.

"He's going to use your fear of him against you," Evan announced.

"I'm not afraid of him," Skye replied.

Ricca held still. Her wolf demanded she go to their mate. The faint scent of fear permeated the air.

It was a lie.

Ricca swallowed hard and glanced at Decker who was staring at her. She blinked and broke the staring contest and turned her attention back to Skye.

She was going to have to come clean with her cousin.

"Hmmm..." Evan stood tall. The strength of him radiated through the air.

Her wolf paused her pacing, sensing her alpha was not pleased with her presence. Evan gazed at her; his hard eyes narrowed on her. Ricca immediately lowered her eyes to the floor.

"Is there anything that I should know?" Evan asked. "I don't want to be caught off guard."

Ricca's gaze flicked to her alpha. What was he trying to insinuate? The alpha stared at Skye who shook her head. Ricca stepped forward, but Decker's hand shot out and rested against her stomach to keep her from moving.

He shook his head

"There's nothing else for me to tell. Everything I've shared with you before was the truth. Barone is a monster," Skye snapped. Her voice was hard and fierce. "That wolf was the cause of—"

She stopped, her body slumping back into the chair. She appeared defeated. Her head hung low, her dark hair cascading forward, blocking her face from view.

Ricca's wolf growled low.

Their mate needed them.

"He caused what?" Evan asked quietly.

"I know without a doubt Barone had my bother killed. I don't have proof, but I know with everything inside me that my brother's death was because of my relationship with Reade." Skye's body shook. She held on to Rolf who was fussing slightly.

Ricca strode forward, ignoring her cousin's command. She moved to Skye and knelt on the floor by her. She rested her hands on Skye's knees and squeezed them.

Skye lifted her head slightly, her chin resting on Rolf's shoulder.

The pain in her eyes struck Ricca down to her core.

"Don't worry. We will take care of everything." Ricca murmured.

"This is just too painful. He's taken everything from me." Tears streamed down Skye's face.

The pain in the brown orbs had Ricca's wolf frantic to get out. Her animal wanted to go after the wolf who had brought this pain to her mate. She wanted to kill Barone Westway.

"He can't have my baby," Skye said.

Ricca tightened her grip on Skye's knees.

"He won't." Ricca made the promise, and she was going to keep it. "You are no longer alone. You have me."

Skye bit her lip and nodded. Her hand slipped down and covered Ricca's.

A knock sounded at the door.

"It is time," Evan announced.

Ricca stood and held out her hand for Skye. She hefted Rolf onto her hip. They entwined their fingers. Ricca ignored the curious glances of her cousin and the alpha. If they had any questions of what was going on between her and Skye, she would answer them later.

Now they had much bigger problems.

The confrontation with Barone.

Even though it was a virtual call, Skye trembled as if she were walking to a room to face Barone in person. Ricca tightened her grip on Skye's hand. She wasn't going anywhere, and she would lend every ounce of strength she could give her.

SKYE TOOK the seat at the table and held on to Rolfie. His squeal filled the air. Ricca couldn't help but smile at the baby's laughter. The alpha took the seat next to Skye while his assistant fiddled with the computer monitor.

"Come here." Decker grabbed Ricca's elbow and pulled her from the room.

She glanced back over her shoulder briefly and took in Skye's small form.

Decker closed the door and gently pushed her against the wall.

"Why are you dragging me out here?" she exclaimed. She brushed her hair from her face and blew out an exasperated breath.

"What is going on with you and the girl?" Decker folded his arms in front of his massive chest. Her cousin leveled a serious gaze on her.

Ricca swallowed hard and met his look. Her wolf paced back and forth, a low growl emanating from her. She clenched her fists together and shut her eyes. She tried to will her animal to stand down.

This was her cousin.

He was on their side.

He wouldn't come between her and her mate.

"Skye is my mate."

Decker swore and stepped back automatically as if she had hit him. "Seriously?"

"I wouldn't play around with something like this." Ricca leaned back against the wall. She rubbed her hands on her jeans and blew out a shaky breath. The urge to go back in the room with Skye was strong. Her wolf wanted to protect her and Rolfie. Her animal had connected to his, and the little pup was defenseless, and his crazy grandfather was on the hunt for him.

"Does the alpha know?" Her cousin stepped forward and rested his hand on her shoulder.

"I'm sure he does now." A small smile played on her lips thinking of the look the alpha had shot her when he'd caught her scent on Skye. The thought of being able to scream to the world that she had found the one person who was made for her excited her.

"Does she know?" A single eyebrow of his rose in question.

"Sort of."

"What is that supposed to mean?"

"We just haven't had a chance to openly talk about it." She shrugged. Her long strands fell forward again. She reached inside her jeans pocket and brought out a tie. She arranged her hair up into a messy bun on top of her head.

"Your scent is all over her." He chuckled and patted her on the shoulder. "Better question to ask, have you informed your parents you've found your mate?"

"Not yet. It all kind of happened fast since this was my assignment. When this is all over, I plan to take Skye and Rolf to their home so I can introduce them." Ricca felt a bit guilty she hadn't called her parents. Roger and Cinder Radcliff were going to get a kick out of not only gaining a daughter-in-law but a grandchild as well.

"Come. Let's go back in, but you need to have that conversation with your mate soon." He motioned for her to go back into the office.

"We will as soon as we get back to the cabin today." She wasn't going to wait any longer. She needed to speak with Skye and get everything off her chest. Her animal wanted to claim Skye and make Rolf her own son as well.

The sooner she could sink her fangs into Skye's flesh the better. No shifter could go against the mating bite.

They reentered the room, and Ricca stalked toward Skye.

"Let me take Rolf. We can so sit over by the windowsill where he won't be in the view of the camera." She knelt by Skye and held her hands out.

Rolf grinned at her and leaned toward her with his arms outstretched.

"Thanks." Skye wiped her hands on her leggings and offered Ricca a smile.

Rolf giggled and rested his head against Ricca's chest. Her wolf reached out to his smaller one. It was playful and curious.

"Come on, little guy. We're not going to go too far from Mommy." She dropped a kiss on the top of his head. Her wolf pushed forward, wanting to get to the baby. The animal was just as protective of Rolf as she was of Skye.

"We are good to go," Alise announced. She tapped a few commands on the keyboard, straightening to her full height.

Decker settled in next to her. He held a finger

out toward Rolf who took it and immediately tried to pull it over to his mouth.

Decker chuckled and drew his hand back.

Rolf had won over her cousin.

"When you're ready, all you have to do is click here," Anise gave instructions to the alpha. She placed the mouse on the table in front of him and Skye. "Mr. Westway is already logged in waiting for you."

"Thanks, Anise." The alpha nodded to her.

She bowed her head and scurried from the room.

The tension thickened and became stifling.

"Are you ready for this?" The alpha turned toward Skye.

"I want this over. I want to start my new life here in Howling Valley with my child. I can't keep looking over my shoulder, afraid that my son will be taken from me." Skye sat taller in her chair. Her voice was firm and steady.

Ricca was so proud of her. Her mate was strong, and they would get through this.

"All right then." Evan reached over and took the mouse in his hand. A few clicks later, and the screen popped open.

A big burly man with olive skin, tousled thick,

dark hair, and hard eyes appeared.

Ricca's breath caught in her throat.

Those eyes were the same as Rolf's.

Only his were unyielding with an evil glare while Rolf's were wide and innocent.

Her wolf instantly went on alert. This was the man who wanted to take Rolf from her and Skye.

"You have something that belongs to me." The low baritone of his voice sent a ripple of tremors down Ricca's spine. He leaned forward with a snarl. "And I want it back."

CHAPTER TWELVE

Skye gripped the arms of the chair. Barone appeared larger than life before her.

She would not show fear.

He was on the computer screen and could not touch her. His snarl marred his face that once would have been considered handsome. Reade had resembled his father, and unfortunately, Rolf was already sharing some of their facial characteristics.

"My son is not a thing," she snapped.

"Be quiet, woman. Let the men in the room talk." Barone turned his attention to Evan. "Alpha." He gave a slight nod to Evan. The only thing

Barone respected was other men in power. His treatment of women was horrific. He had no respect for women except for what they could do for a man and to breed them for the next generation.

"Alpha."

Skye wished she had an ounce of Evan's confidence. He didn't blink while participating in the virtual stare off. She was grateful that Ricca had the suggestion of removing Rolf from the view of the camera. She was sure Barone's attention would only be on the baby.

"As I said, you have something of mine in your possession. My grandson, my heir, who is the future leader of my pack, and he needs to be returned where he belongs," Barone announced.

"He belongs with his mother," Skye interjected. He was not going to ignore her. This was her son they were speaking of. Not a possession.

Not a toy or an inanimate object.

They were talking of a little boy.

An innocent baby.

Who belonged with her.

"Shut it, woman." He growled.

She jerked back from the hate burning in his eyes. It was as if she were struck down by his hand.

The sound of low growling in the corner of the room was heard.

"I don't know what my son saw in you, a human —"

"Now you won't talk to a member of my pack like that." Evan's low voice sliced through the air. He leaned forward. The power of his alpha waves flowed around her like a warm breeze. She may not be a shifter, but even she sensed how strong Evan was.

"Now you see here. You don't want to fuck with my pack—"

"I'm not worried about your little pack," Evan cut him off.

He leveled his gaze on the monitor, and if Barone was actually in front of them, she was sure he would have been knocked back by Evan's power.

"Skye Lennon is under my protection, as is her child, and you will not continue to bother her."

"You can't just claim my grandson as a member of your pack, and you know that," Barone hollered. His fangs were evident as he sneered. "Have you forgot about the laws set by the council? The boy belongs with his pack. He's not old enough to make the decision, and his father's blood determines where he belongs."

"That can't be!" Skye gasped. She turned to Evan, praying that Barone was incorrect. Her body practically trembled with fear as it encompassed her.

Evan glared at the screen but didn't offer a rebuttal.

There was no way in hell she would give up her child. Humans had to have some right. "You lie!"

Barone threw his head back and barked hefty laughter.

This can't be true. She was Rolf's mother and she'd fight any council to save her child. Her mind immediately raced. She was going to have to find a pricy lawyer. One she wasn't going to be able to afford. She didn't care what she would have to do, even if she had to sell her soul to the Devil, she would do so to protect her baby boy.

"You've laid with wolves and yet you still know nothing about our kind or way. Go ahead. Ask your new alpha. He'll tell you I speak the truth." Barone settled back in his chair with a stupid grin on his face.

Skye had never been one to promote violence, but at that moment she would have gladly tried to kill Barone Westway.

This was the first time she'd heard of some

council. Would they really side with Barone just because Rolf was half a shifter? What about his human side?

"Don't worry, Skye. We'll submit an official appeal to revoke his rights." Evan's eyes were somber.

Skye pushed back from the chair and stood abruptly. The room whirled. She tried to inhale but was struggling to breathe.

This couldn't be happening.

"I'm going to give you a little time to let this sink in. My next call will be to discuss handing over my grandson."

The screen went black.

Arms closed around her and pulled her in close.

Ricca.

Skye melted into her while her body shook from the sobs that poured from her.

"Shhh..." Ricca's lips brushed her forehead. Her hold tightened on Skye.

The warmth of her body was comforting, but it didn't take away the fact that Barone held some claim on her son.

"He can't have Rolf," Skye whimpered. Her hands closed into fists, gripping Ricca's shirt. She eased back away from Ricca and spun around. She didn't care about the tears marring her face. Her gaze landed on Rolf in Decker's arms. "I won't give my son to that monster."

"We can go to the council," Ricca said. "There has to be some loophole in the laws."

"It's a chance we can take." Evan stood and snagged his phone from the table. "There is a council meeting tomorrow. When together they hear out discrepancies amongst the wolf community."

Skye felt some form of hope. She smiled up at Ricca through her tears. The conversation they sort of had in the car allowed her to see what she had known all along.

She and Ricca were destined mates.

This woman was not willing to roll over and bow down to the other alpha. She was willing to fight at Skye's side.

"We will go and beg the council if we have to." Ricca took Skye's hand in hers. She brought it up to her lips and kissed it. "I will do everything in my power to keep Rolfie with us."

Skye nodded and stepped closer to Ricca.

"Thank you," Skye whispered. She didn't know what she would do without this woman, and she never wanted to find out.

This was where she belonged.

Ricca was hers.

"You don't have to thank me, mate."

Skye's breath was ripped from her.

Confirmation of what she had known all along. Tears blurred her vision. She reached up and wrapped her arms around Ricca's neck and guided her head down to hers for a short kiss.

Skye didn't care that they weren't the only ones in the room. She would never shy away from showing her affection to the woman she had fallen in love with.

"Ricca, the two of you will need to leave tomorrow morning to ensure you arrive in time. The council will arrive tomorrow night in Aston. You will need to be there."

Decker walked over to them and held out Rolf to Skye. She took her son and brought him close to her. Having Ricca's arms around her while holding on to her son was comforting. She kissed his chubby cheeks and inhaled his scent. This was her child, and no one was going to take him from her. She glanced up at Ricca and blew out a heavy breath.

Deep down inside, she knew they had to make the trip. If they had to speak with this council to get permission for her to keep her son, then it was something she would have to do.

She had no other choice.

"What do I need to pack?"

RICCA GLANCED BACK into the alpha house. Skye had remained inside with Jena while she had stepped outside to speak with her cousin.

"Are you sure you don't want someone to go with you?" he asked.

She sat on the bottom step and shook her head. "We'll be fine. I think we'll be able to move quicker with just the two of us. Maybe we can leave Rolf here—"

"Having the baby with you will help. Play to the council's weakness. A mother and her baby." Decker slid his hands into his jeans pocket. He kicked at a rock on the ground that was near his boots.

"That makes sense." She really hadn't wanted to take the baby with them. She had hoped to leave him secured, but if Decker thought it was best, then she would take him with them. They were going to need use everything they had to make the council see that Rolf belonged with his mother.

And her.

The Nightstar Pack was strong and respectable. With Evan welcoming Skye into their pack, it would show the council that Skye planned to stay with shifters which would be vital to a growing young male wolf.

And once they had mated, it would confirm her loyalty to wolves.

"I can see the bond between the two of you. Don't wait too long to claim her." Decker grinned. "And to think your mate basically was handed to you. I'm going to have to tell the alpha to give me a protection detail. Maybe I'll find my mate that way."

"You never know," she teased.

Decker was a good man who deserved to find his mate and start a family. It was something every wolf she knew longed for.

Ricca pushed off the stairs and moved to Decker. He opened his arms and enclosed them around her. He was like the big brother she'd never had, and it felt good to be able to share in the excitement of finding her mate. She was going to have to call her parents and tell them. She wasn't going to have time to take Skye and Rolf to them before they had to meet with the council, but once this was all over, she was going to introduce them to each other.

"I'm so happy for you." He dropped a kiss on the top of her head.

She stepped away and exhaled.

"You are doing a damn good job as an enforcer," he said. "When this is all over, we'll have plenty more exciting things for you to do."

"Thanks." She pushed her hair behind her ear. The memory of her finding the scent of an unknown wolf came to mind. "By any chance have you sent anyone out to our cabin to patrol?"

"No. Why?" Decker frowned.

"I was patrolling last night and caught the scent of a wolf I didn't recognize. I wasn't sure if you had someone come out to check in on us."

"I would have notified you if I did so that you wouldn't have been caught off guard." He narrowed his gaze on her. He was now officially in his enforcer mode. "Maybe we should send someone out—"

"No, it's fine. It was only in one area. It could have been someone passing. The scent never went near the house but stayed in the woods." She didn't want them thinking she couldn't handle this. Maybe she shouldn't have mentioned this. For all she knew it could have been someone from the pack who she didn't know, out for a run. "If I need help, I'll call you. I promise."

"That's a given. You better call if you run into trouble. It doesn't matter what time of day or night it is. Me and all the enforcers will have your back."

Ricca nodded. This had been stressed during her training. She would never be alone.

"When you get back to the cabin, do a quick sweep of the property. If you detect the scent again, you call me."

"Yes, sir." Ricca saluted him.

There was no joking in his tone, and his eyes were dead serious. If there was an outsider lingering around their cabin, they would be hunted down.

CHAPTER TWELVE

Ricca trotted thought the thick foliage. She breathed in the fresh scents of the forest and didn't catch anything out of the ordinary.

They had returned to the cabin after their trip to the alpha's home. They had spent half the day there. Jena had taken a liking to Skye and Rolf. Ricca could tell that Skye missed her mother, and Jena was a great substitute for her. Jena had shared some baby tips with Skye.

She had spoken about them the entire trip back to the cabin. Not that Ricca minded. She didn't know the first thing about babies, so anything she could learn, she would willingly absorb the new information.

Once they returned home, she had sent Skye inside to take care of the fussy Rolf. He had missed his nap due to the excitement at the alpha's home. Everyone who met Rolf became captivated by the little pup. He had the toughest of enforcers getting down on the floor to play with him.

With the amount of people at the alpha's home, there had been no privacy. She and Skye had not had a chance to continue their conversation from earlier.

Ricca increased her speed. She had lost track of time, and the sun was descending. She would need to go pack a bag. She would need to sit Skye down so they could come up with a plan. They needed to be on the same page and discuss what they would speak with the council about.

She paused at a faint noise in the distance. Her enhanced hearing picked up that the noise was a small animal.

Not a wolf.

She breathed a sigh of relief and kept heading toward the cabin. The anticipation of being in

Skye's presence again had her in an almost full-blown sprint. Her paws pounded the ground and ate up the distance.

She had to see her mate.

Ricca arrived at the edge of the trees, and she slowed down. Her ears picked up on another noise. This one was the sound of feet padding across the grass.

Ricca's muscles relaxed. She stepped from the brush and took in the sight of her woman sitting on a blanket in the middle of the yard.

Ricca's heart stuttered.

Skye was naked.

The moon softly caressed Skye's body, and the need to be close to her was overwhelming.

Ricca's paws moved before she knew it. The drive to be by Skye's side took over. She trotted over to Skye, unable to take her eyes off her.

She arrived a few feet away from her mate. She urged her animal to go in the background, but the damn wolf was stubborn. She wanted to greet Skye.

Fine.

Ricca rolled her eyes. She crept forward slowly until she arrived at Skye's side.

Skye's giggles floated through the air. She

reached out and rubbed Ricca on the top of her head. Her fingers dove into Ricca's thick fur.

"You are such a beauty," Skye murmured.

Her animal practically purred at the praise from Skye. She pushed her forehand against Skye's stomach. Skye's finger moved down her neck and stroked her.

Ricca sat back in shock at how her wolf was behaving. Another rumble escaped from Ricca. She was truly enjoying feeling Skye's hands running along her fur.

Okay. It's my turn, Ricca exclaimed. Her beast whined but finally gave in.

Ricca took a few steps back and allowed the change to overcome her. She welcomed the faint pain while her bones reconstructed into her human form. The dark fur disappeared back into her skin. Within a minute she was kneeling on the soft grass, once again a human.

She opened her eyes, and they locked on Skye.

"That is amazing," Skye breathed.

Ricca's gaze roamed Skye's high, full breasts, wide hips, and her creamy skin. A growl escaped her as she crawled over to Skye.

She took her mate by surprise and knocked her

over. Skye's laughter was infectious. Ricca loved hearing it and made a promise to herself that she would do what she must to keep Skye laughing.

They'd be under a tremendous amount of stress come tomorrow.

Tonight would be about them.

"You are beautiful," Skye murmured.

Ricca leaned down and covered Skye's lips with hers. She took her mate's mouth in a deep, passionate kiss. All of the emotions she wanted to say were poured into this one kiss.

Skye's hands came up and threaded their way into Ricca's locks.

Ricca wasn't sure who moaned, her or Skye. The intense heat coiling into Ricca's belly was ready to explode. She had her mate underneath her, out in the open, naked, and there was nothing more she wanted to do but claim her mate.

Her gums stretched and burned from her canines descending. The scent of Skye's arousal greeted her. Ricca tore her lips from Skye's. She inhaled sharply, breathing in the sweet tangy scent.

"I need you," Ricca growled.

"I'm all yours, Ricca." Skye's wide eyes met her. She brandished the creamy column of her neck.

Ricca's heart pounded.

"Are you sure?" Ricca reached out with a trembling hand and trailed her fingers along Skye's soft skin. She had to concentrate and keep from lashing out and sinking her teeth into Skye's flesh. She needed to be absolutely sure Skye knew what she was offering. "Mating is forever. If I bite you, there is no turning back. You will belong to me until the end of time."

Skye slid her foot along the back of Ricca's calf. It was sensual and brought her center directly onto Ricca's lower belly. The scent of her arousal grew.

"Yes." Skye turned back to Ricca. Her hands were buried in Ricca's thick hair and guided her head down to hers. She stopped when their lips were a hair's breadth away from each other. "I'm your mate. Take me."

A growl rippled out of the depths of Ricca's soul. Skye acknowledged what she was to Ricca. This acceptance floored Ricca. Too overcome with emotion, she decided to show Skye how much she meant to her.

She pressed a hard kiss to Skye's lips, taking her by her dark hair and jerking her head to the side.

Ricca buried her face into the crook of Skye's

neck and inhaled the scent of her woman. It was unlike anything she had every breathed in. Skye's breaths were coming fast. Her breasts brushed against Ricca's with every rise and fall of her chest.

She whimpered and rested her hand on the small of Ricca's back.

"I love you," Skye whispered.

Ricca closed her eyes for a moment and opened them. She lifted her head and smiled.

"I love you, too."

Ricca had waited for this moment for a lifetime.

Ricca licked the full length of Skye's neck and shuddered. She never thought in a million years that she would ever find her mate, and now, she had her right where she belonged.

Underneath her.

Ricca raised her head slightly. The moon's rays shined down brightly on them, giving her just the amount of light she needed.

She sank her teeth in the curve of Skye's shoulder. Her mate tensed for a moment but then relaxed back on the blanket. The sweet copper essence of Skye's blood touched her tongue.

Ricca's wolf howled.

Skye cried out as her orgasm ripped its way

through her. The bite of a mate would drive the pleasure senses wild and elicit such a reaction.

A warm sensation rippled its way through Ricca. The wind picked up around them as if the gods above were celebrating their union.

An invisible rope wrapped its way around Ricca's heart.

The bond between wolf and mate was sealed. It was official. They would walk through life together.

Ricca released Skye and licked the wound. Her saliva had proteins in it that would allow her mate to heal. Skye would no longer age as a human, but as a shifter. They would have a long life together.

Skye trembled still as her body accepted Ricca.

Once she was satisfied that the blood had ceased flowing, Ricca lifted her head. She met the shocked gaze of her newly claimed mate.

"I didn't hurt you, did I?" she asked. She was worried slightly since her mate was human.

Skye shook her head. A smile formed on her lips. She reached up and ran a finger along Ricca's bottom lip.

"No, mate, you did not." Skye's breaths were rapid. A fine sheen of sweat coated her body. "How did I climax so fast?"

"It was the claiming."

Ricca grinned and adjusted her body down to where she was eye level with Skye's breasts. She licked and teased them. They were Ricca's second favorite part of Skye. She took her time suckling them and drinking in the nourishing fluid that seeped from them.

Ricca moved on, trailing kisses along Skye's body. Her mate writhed on the blanket underneath her. Ricca wanted to kiss and lick every inch of the woman who now belonged to her. She made her way to Skye's center and pushed her legs apart.

Ricca groaned as the scent of her mate's arousal was overwhelming. She parted Skye's folds and trailed her tongue through Skye's soaked slit. She arrived at Skye's clitoris and bathed it with her tongue. She drew it into her mouth and suckled it.

Skye's back arched from the ground.

"Ricca!" she cried out.

Ricca was pleased to hear her mate calling her name while she feasted on her. She increased her pressure on Skye's clit while introducing two fingers inside her mate. Skye's slick channel was snug and stretched around Ricca's fingers.

She thrust inside Skye hard while focusing on her clit. Ricca closed her eyes, basking in the wonders that were before her. She couldn't get enough of Skye, and the taste of her was captivating.

Skye was close to reaching her second orgasm.

Ricca vowed right then under the moon that she would forever protect this woman, cherish her, give her pleasure, and would forever walk by her side.

Skye's hips bucked underneath her. Ricca continued with her sweet torture of her mate. She twisted her fingers around to find that certain spot that would send her mate to the heavens. Skye's body shook, and she wasn't going to last much longer.

Her thighs closed in around Ricca's head. Skye's hands found their way to Ricca's hair in a painful grip. Ricca couldn't care less if she were bald by morning.

"Ricca!" Skye called out again. Her muscles tightened, and she exploded. Her hips flew off the ground while she strained against Ricca's hand. Skye's warm channel clenched around Ricca's fingers.

Her release slipped from her center. Ricca lapped up the creamy goodness, pleased that her mate was able to reach her climax.

Skye flopped back down on the blanket, her

breaths coming out in hard pants. Ricca withdrew her fingers and promptly cleaned them off. She cleaned up all of the evidence of Skye's orgasm.

"I love you so much." Skye sighed.

"And I you." Ricca was humbled by the love of this woman. She kissed Skye's inner thigh then crawled over Skye. She braced herself over the woman she loved and grinned down at her. "What were you doing out here?"

"Waiting on you."

Ricca rewarded her with a kiss. She couldn't wait to see what the future held. She hoped her mate would continue to find ways to greet her properly when she came home. She couldn't wait to move Skye and Rolf into her home.

But before they moved into the future, they had to settle Skye's past.

Ricca lay down on the blanket next to Skye who rolled over and pressed her soft body to hers. She rested her head in the crook of Ricca's arm.

Ricca couldn't have asked for anything more perfect. They lay there, no words were needed. The moon was high, and the sounds of nature surrounded them. There was no other place Ricca would rather be.

Skye's hand skated across Ricca's belly. She drew small symbols and snuggled closer.

"Did you know I was your mate when we first met?" Skye's voice broke the comfortable silence.

"From the moment I laid eyes on you, I knew," Ricca admitted. She remembered the moment vividly.

"Really? I figured there was going to be something between us from the moment we shook hands."

Ricca glanced at her, surprised. Her mate had felt the bond between them.

Skye chuckled. "Everything about you turned me on. I just knew you would scent that I was aroused."

"I scented it. It was torture driving to the cabin."

"Torture?" Skye gasped.

"Yes. I wanted to pull the truck over, find a little secluded spot, and fuck you."

Skye grew quiet. Her hand moved up to Ricca's breast and slowly played with her hardened nipple.

"Maybe you should have," she whispered.

A growl rumbled from Ricca's chest. Her animal liked the sound of that. She would keep that in mind for the future. Spontaneous sex with her mate would be the best. Skye kissed her cheek. Her hand slid back to rest on Ricca's stomach. They continued to lie underneath the wide-open night sky.

The sounds of the forest were magical. It heightened the atmosphere of love surrounding Ricca and Skye.

"How can I claim you?" she asked.

A tiny smile appeared on Ricca's lips. She leaned down and kissed Skye's forehead.

"I'm not sure. Your bite wouldn't be deep enough to leave a lasting mark. I heal too quickly."

Skye pouted, and Ricca instantly felt bad. She ran a hand along Skye's back and kissed her lips. They could think of ways for Skye to claim her. Maybe they could think of the traditional way of humans with a wedding.

"Believe me, mate. There won't be a wolf around who won't know I belong to you." She grinned.

"How so?" Skye arched one of her eyebrows high.

Ricca ran a hand down Skye's hip to her thighs. She pushed Skye's legs open and slipped her fingers between Skye's slit. She groaned at the feeling of Skye's pussy that was still wet.

Skye gasped and allowed her legs to fall open. Her eyes widened when Ricca pushed a finger inside her. The warmth of her core greeted Ricca.

She quickly pulled her finger out and brought it to her lips. She licked it slowly, Skye's eyes tracking her tongue.

"They will scent you on me." Ricca grinned again. This was one scent that she would be proud to wear. She planned to feast on her mate daily. Her sweet nectar was addicting, and she couldn't get enough of her mate orgasming on her tongue and shouting her name to the heavens.

Skye laughed and pushed Ricca back onto the ground. She braced herself over Ricca with a twinkle in her eyes.

"Is that so?" She planted a kiss on Ricca lips. Trailed kisses along Ricca's chin, chest, and down to her stomach.

Ricca parted her legs to allow Skye to settle between them. Her mate licked her lips as she stared down at her pussy. Ricca needed to feel her mate's tongue on her.

"Then I'll have to make sure they are able to do the same with me," Skye said.

"What is that?" Ricca moaned.

Skye took one long lick of her. A shudder

rippled its way through Ricca. She gripped Skye's hair and guided her back to her center. She lifted her hips to meet her mate's mouth. Her clit pulsed with need.

Skye paused and locked her gaze with Ricca.

"Making sure they can smell you on me."

CHAPTER FOURTEEN

Ricca had woken Skye with a kiss that took her breath away. If waking up next to this woman every day was going to be like this, then Skye was in Heaven. They slowly got dressed, remaining quiet.

Today she would have to face reality that there was a chance she would lose her son. They quickly got the truck packed up.

Rolf, even though he was only a baby, must have sensed something was afoot. It would been the wolf in him that recognized the tension in the air.

Once they were ready, they had taken off,

leaving the town of Howling Valley behind and headed toward Aston, Utah.

They had been driving in silence for a while. Skye prayed to whatever gods were listening that the council would side with her. It would be cruel to snatch a young babe from his mother.

They had crossed over into Nevada hours ago. Skye reached for her window and rolled it down farther. The warm air filled the truck. She winced slightly, her shoulder still sore.

"Are you in pain?" Ricca asked.

Skye wasn't sure how Ricca detected her discomfort. She hadn't taken her eyes off the road in some time.

"Nothing I can't deal with."

Ricca reached for Skye's hand and brought it to her lips. Her kiss provided some comfort for Skye. Without a doubt, Ricca would stand beside her.

"Everything is going to work out in our favor. The council will hear us out and agree that Rolfie belongs with us." Ricca glanced over at Skye. She entwined their fingers together and rested their clasped hands on her lap.

It warmed Skye's heart to hear Ricca claim Rolf. Her son may have lost a father, but he'd gained another mother. Another person who would love him and treat him as her own.

Skye couldn't have asked for a better mate. She tightened her grip on Ricca's hand.

"He's our baby."

"He is, and he will grow up to be a strong wolf and find his place in the Nightstar Pack and the world."

As if to agree, Rolf let out a string of babbling.

They shared a laugh. Skye relaxed slightly. If Ricca had faith, then she would, too.

"So, this council. Who is it made up of?" she asked, curious.

Barone had been right about one thing. For as long as she had lived amongst the wolves of Half Moon Bay, she had never heard of such a council.

"It is a group of elders who are old and wise. They oversee things in our society such as our laws and our history. They were created centuries ago to protect wolves. They are highly respected, and no one would dare go against them. That's why we need their blessing to keep Rolf with us. If they side with us, then there is nothing legally Barone could do. If he goes against the council, then he will have to deal with them, and there is no alpha in their right mind who would do so."

Skye snorted. Barone was insane, and he would be the one alpha who would defy authority.

"I wouldn't put it past Barone. He will do what he must to get what he wants."

"And then he will be punished by the council. Our society dates back for at least a millennium. The power they wield will quench whatever deranged delusions he has in that small brain of his." Ricca grinned.

There weren't any cars around on the deserted Nevada highway. The sky was bluer than anything Skye had ever seen before. It looked as if someone had painted it. The few clouds were bright-white and perfect. The wonders of nature never failed to amaze Skye.

She breathed in the fresh air.

Today would be the first day of their new life. She was going to meet with this council and plead her case.

A small shred of doubt was hiding in the back of her mind.

"But what if they don't side with us. What if they decide being with Barone is best for Rolf?" Skye stared off into the desert, not wanting to look at Ricca. Just the thought of not having her child with her speared a sharp pain in her chest. She wouldn't know what she would do without her son. He was her world. There was a connection between a mother and son that was undeniable.

Would they strip her son from her and give him to that monster?

"I'm sure the council knows of Barone and all of the things he has done. I've looked into him, and I'm surprised he's even still alive."

"What do you mean?" Skye's attention flew to Ricca.

"That some other wolf hasn't taken him out. He's a tyrant and has done so much wrong. I'm a firm believer that fate will do unto him what he has done to others."

The image of her brother came to mind. Gabe had been her rock. Ever since their parents had died, it had been just the two of them. His death had left a hole in her heart, and she knew Barone was involved. She was sure it was his way of trying to control her. He'd never come out and admitted it, but it would make sense.

She'd given birth to the future. At the time Reade was still alive, so he had been the heir. His father may not have wanted them together, but the moment she'd birthed Rolf, that all changed.

When Reade died, his interest grew.

She swallowed hard. She was never one to wish bad things on people, but she prayed Barone would have to atone for all of his sins.

She glanced at the beautiful sky again and imagined her family watching over her and Rolf. She just wished her parents and brother had been able to meet Rolf.

They would have loved him fiercely and spoiled him rotten.

"How much longer?" Skye asked. Her breast had grown heavy, signaling it was time to feed her babe.

"Little under two hours. We don't have far to go once we cross over into Utah."

"Okay." She undid her seatbelt and crawled into the back.

She sat next to Rolf who eyed her. He offered her a grin, showcasing his two tiny bottom teeth. He grew excited and danced in his seat. The boy knew what time it was.

Feeding time.

She unbuttoned then opened her shirt. She freed her first breast and felt a heated gaze on her.

She flicked her gaze to the rearview mirror and was met with Ricca's glowing amber eyes.

Skye smiled and reached for Rolf. He immediately wrestled his way down onto her lap and latched on to her.

A popular song came on the radio. Ricca turned it up and sang off-key with it.

Skye smiled. She currently had everything she wanted. A woman who loved her, her son, and a second chance at happiness. She couldn't ask for anything better.

She just prayed the trip home would be the same.

"COME THIS WAY." Ricca guided her toward a building she would have assumed would have been hidden deep in the woods. Aston was a shifter town. According to Ricca, there were a handful of humans who resided there, and they, too, worked for the council.

Skye had Rolf against her chest. He was curious by nature and was taking in the scenery around them.

The sinister-looking brick, two-story structure could have been right out of a fantasy movie. Large stone wolves graced the roof on the corners as if they were guarding it. Upon the sides, random areas were covered in thick vines.

Rolf whined and tried to pull away from her. She exhaled and loosened her grip on him. Ricca directed them toward the main entrance. The doors were massive wood structures.

Two oversized men stood before them. They had to be shifters. Skye swallowed hard and followed Ricca up the few stairs that led toward the men. Once they arrived at the landing, Skye moved closer to Ricca. They were even larger up close. The dark-haired one had to be pushing seven feet tall, while the blond stood a few inches shorter. They had broad shoulders and were dressed in leather with weapons visibly placed along their bodies.

They had to be enforcers.

"Greetings." Ricca nodded to them.

"State your business." The dark-haired one's voice was unbelievably low.

His dark, piercing eyes landed on Skye. Had she been alone, she would have turned tail and ran away.

"We are here to seek the council's ear," Ricca announced. She stood tall. Her voice was firm and steady. Her long silvery hair fluttered in the slight breeze that blew past them.

"What pack do you represent?" he asked.

"The Nightstar. Evan Gerwulf is my alpha."

He flicked his gaze to the blond guard who gave a slight tilt of his head.

"You may enter." He grabbed the handle and opened the door. He faced them again and waited for them to cross over the threshold.

"Come. It's okay." Ricca rested her hand at the small of Skye's back and urged her on.

Skye nodded and walked along with her. They entered and were in a foyer with a chandelier hanging from the ceiling and old paintings lining the wall. There were photos of wolves and men. They strolled down the short hall that ended with two paths for them to take.

"This way."

"How do you know where to go?" Skye asked. A nervous chuckle escaped her. She glanced around and tried to take in their surroundings. Everything was old. Skye would guess the building had to have been around for over two hundred years. The decor was that of the nineteenth century.

"I can hear people talking."

They took the right hallway, and soon Skye was greeted with a line at a door.

She flicked her gaze to Ricca who had a devilish grin on her lips. Skye rolled her eyes.

Wolves and their hearing.

They arrived at the end of the line where there were only a few people ahead of them.

"We are early," Ricca murmured.

"Anyone can come to the council with their problems?" Skye asked.

"Yup." Ricca moved closer as a man left the room.

He was burly and looked like a wolf. His hair was thick and crazed. His amber-eyed gaze landed on Skye. Ricca issued a low warning growl. He tore his eyes from Skye and continued past them.

"What was that?" Skye wasn't sure what had just passed between Ricca and the other shifter. Wolves were very territorial, and she assumed that was Ricca's way of warning him from her.

"Nothing." Ricca rested an arm around her waist.

Yup.

A wolf territorial thing.

"The council holds public hearings where any

wolf shifter can come and share their issues, worries, and needs to them."

Skye moved closer to Ricca, enjoying the feel of her warmth.

Rolf innocently babbled in her arms while they waited. The woman in front of them rotated around. She smiled at Rolf who greeted her with a wide grin. He laughed, and all around them smiled and gave him attention.

Soon, it was their turn to enter the room. Butterflies appeared in Skye's stomach. She tightened her hold on Rolf and sent a prayer up to the heavens.

The council had to side with them.

Ricca took her hand and threaded their fingers together. She guided Skye into the chamber. Had it not been for her, Skye may have changed her mind and run away.

A chill slid down her spine.

A slight draft blew. The room was dark with lit sconces lining the walls. She felt as if she had been transported back in time. Skye squeezed her grip on Ricca's hand. She needed to draw on her strength. She was barely able to put one foot in front of the other.

They walked along a dark carpet that led to a

table. Six members of the council sat in high-backed chairs behind a monstrous table. Goblets rested in front of each member.

Four men and two women.

This was who would determine the fate of her son.

For them to be elders, Skye had been prepared to speak with ancient-looking people, but alas, they were anything but. The men appeared tall and strong while the women were slightly smaller, but Skye was sure they were a force like the men. She assumed to be a member of such an esteemed group, one would have had to prove themselves.

Power radiated from the group. It didn't take one of the paranormal world to sense it. Skye swallowed hard. She held her head up high for she knew they would detect she was human. Her son quieted and twisted his head to get a look at the people before them.

They stopped at the edge of the carpet.

"Ricca Radcliffe, enforcer for the Nightstar Pack," the councilmen sitting at the center of the group bellowed. He wore a dark robe, as did all of them. His hair, the color of midnight, hung along his shoulders in waves. His tanned skin was smooth, and his eyes burned amber.

"Councilmen Dowers." Ricca nodded.

"And who is this human you have with you?" he asked.

The council members glanced at each other. Skye watched, appalled, as they each sniffed the air.

Could they smell Ricca on her that easily?

"This is Skye Lennon," Ricca introduced her.

"She's your mate," one of the women noted. She had long blonde hair pulled up in a high bun.

Skye's question was answered. They must have scented them on each other.

"Yes, Councilwoman Linota, she is." Ricca smiled at her.

Skye drummed up the strength to do the same. The butterflies were growing in her stomach.

"And the babe?" a man, who appeared the oldest and wisest of the group, asked. His locks were held back from his face. His amber eyes were a stark contrast to his deep-brown skin.

"May I introduce to you Rolf Westway." Ricca's smile disappeared.

"Westway? As in the Blackmane pack?" Dowers questioned.

"Yes, sir. My son's father was the late Reade Westway." Skye's voice trembled. She released

Ricca's hand and stepped forward. She positioned Rolf so they could see her son.

"I'm sorry for your loss, my dear. Reade was special," the other woman spoke up. Her flaming-red hair was arranged in intricate braids. She offered a warm smile to Skye.

"Are you telling me that we have the heir to the Blackmane pack before us?" the deep voice from the short-haired councilman broke through the air.

"Yes, Councilman Hiro." Ricca stood to her full height and folded her hands behind her.

"And how is it the heir to the Blackmane pack and his mother stand before us with an enforcer of the Nightstar?" Dowers leaned back in his chair.

"We've come to you due to certain issues that have been brought to—"

"Let Miss Lennon speak," the dark-skinned councilman interjected, cutting Ricca off.

"Yes, Councilman Parkway." Ricca turned to Skye and bowed her head. "It's okay, mate. Tell them everything."

"Everything?" Skye's eyes widened. She glanced at them and didn't know if she could trust them with her troubles with Barone. Would they side with their own kind?

Evan and Ricca wouldn't have had her come to the council if they didn't trust them.

"Please, my dear. What you bring to the council will be kept in confidence. I'm sure there is nothing you can share about Barone Westway that we aren't already aware of," Linota said, apparently picking up on Skye's internal battle.

"This is a safe space, Miss Lennon." Markway's expression softened. He motioned for her to begin.

Skye hefted Rolf up high so he could rest on her hip. His attention was captured by the council. There was something about them that fascinated him.

Skye exhaled and began to speak. She told them of her time in Half Moon Bay, her relationship with Reade, her suspicions of her brother's death, and how the town was run under Barone's ruling.

"And you fled the Blackmane pack because you were in fear of your life?" the other councilwoman, whose name Skye had learned was Estella, asked.

"Yes, ma'am. He's been on a vicious tangent to get me to turn my son over to him. He says that it's the law of the shifters and because of his blood running through Rolf, that he belongs with him." Skye's voice trembled. She had paraphrased

Barone's threats, but she was sure they got the point.

Ricca wrapped an arm around her. It was a welcome move. Skye was seconds from losing it. Thinking how she may lose her son was tearing her apart. Nothing in the world could replace him.

"Calm down. It's okay," Ricca murmured.

"Please tell me that monster isn't correct!" Skye cried out. Tears streamed down her cheeks. She didn't care if she looked crazed or desperate. This was her son's life they were speaking about.

Rolf whined and gripped her shirt. He must have sensed something was wrong.

Her life.

They couldn't take him away from her.

"Centuries ago, a law was developed when wolves were still defining their territories," Markway began. He stood from his seat and stepped around the table.

Skye tightened her hold on Rolf as the councilman walked toward them.

"I'm sure my colleagues can agree that the law you mentioned is old and outdated. No longer are wolves battling each other. In our past, we fought to set boundaries. Packs were at war with each other. That was the time when we had to ensure strong family lines did not die out." He leveled his gaze on her.

"He is correct, my dear. There is a law that supports his claim," Dowers included. He sighed and rested back in his chair. "But as Markway eluded, those days when this law was drafted are no more."

Skye's heart skipped a beat. She frantically eyed all the council members as they spoke low amongst each other. Markway stood in front of her, blocking her view.

"You recently completed the mating bond, I see." His gazed dropped down to Skye's shoulder.

She swallowed hard and glanced over at Ricca who stood proud.

"Yes, sir. We have."

"And you are happy with the Nightstar Pack?" He raised an eyebrow high. He kept his attention on her and didn't look over at Ricca.

"They have been very welcoming to me and my son. The alpha, Evan, is wonderful. I feel safe amongst him and his pack." She squeezed her son tight in her arms and dropped a kiss on his forehead.

He babbled as if to put in his two cents about their new home.

"And your mate?" He jerked his chin toward Ricca.

Her eyes met Ricca's, and Skye was certain she could not have chosen a better mate for herself or her child. Ricca moved closer to her and rested a hand on the small of her back. Just the feeling of Ricca next to her gave her strength.

"She's perfect for me. As if she were made only for me," Skye breathed.

Ricca's eyes deepened. She reached up and cupped Skye's cheek.

"We were made for each other," Ricca corrected. She grinned at Rolf and tousled his hair. "Fate had planned for us to be together the moment we were born."

Markway had a pleased expression in his eyes. He gave them a nod and strode back to the table where he joined in on the deep conversation.

"Please tell me you can hear them." Skye grabbed Ricca's hand. She hadn't thought the council would start having this discussion right in front of them. She guessed it was better than being sent away for days to await their decision.

"Yeah. They are saying this should have been something addressed a long time ago." Ricca paused. She pulled Skye close and kissed her lips. "Don't worry. Have faith."

"I swear I wish I had your hearing," Skye muttered. She had to inject some humor into the matter, or she was going to go insane. They shared a chuckle and tried to act inconspicuous, but she was sure they would know Ricca could hear them.

"Now they are talking about Barone, and it would appear he's been on their radar." Ricca took her hand and entwined their fingers.

Hope blossomed in Skye's chest. If they knew what type of a monster Barone was, then there was a chance they would side with them. Rolf fussed and wiggled around in her arms.

"Here, I can take him." Ricca held out her hands to him.

Rolf practically jumped into her arms. He squealed and laughed, happy to be with Ricca. Skye smiled. She and her son had something in common.

The council continued to speak, and Skye grew even more nervous. Ricca tried to distract her with Rolf. They played with him, and he laughed and giggled. He thrived under the attention and took advantage of it. Ricca's gaze flicked over her shoulder. The muscles on the side of her cheek flexed.

Skye turned around and found the eyes of the

council on them. Their silence was deafening. Skye moved closer to Ricca and reached for her hand.

"Wolf shifters have been an evolving species since the beginning of time. We are a strong race and have been through trying times." Mayday faced them with his hands folded in front of him. He stood regal, his robes brushing the floor. His amber eyes were burning bright as if to signal his wolf was nearby.

Ricca appeared calm, so Skye tried to not panic. If Ricca wasn't then she would follow her lead.

"Many wolves were killed during wars over the past few centuries, and we did what we thought was best to preserve our people." He paused and looked over his shoulder.

Dowers gave a slight nod.

"We realize the ways of the old are not what is best for our people now and we vow today that we are going to review our outdated laws," Mayday said.

Skye squeezed Ricca's hand tight.

Her heart all but leaped up into her throat.

Was he about to say what she had hoped for?

"Thank you, sir," Ricca said.

"I'm sure wolves everywhere will be appreciative of this." Skye tried not to show her impatience. She just needed to know about her son.

What was the damn decision?

"We, the council, have decided that the babe shall stay with his mother."

Skye cried out with joy. She faced Ricca who collapsed onto her where they hugged with poor Rolf trapped between them. He didn't know what was going on and looked to both of his mothers.

"Thank you." Skye sniffed. She spun to the council and took a step forward. She wiped her face with the back of her hand, unable to believe they were agreeing with her. It seemed surreal.

"I'm not finished," Mayday announced. His facial expression was unreadable.

Fear gripped Skye.

What else could there be?

"On the day of the child's eighteenth birthday, he will be given the choice of where he will want to be. He is the rightful heir of the Blackmane pack."

"What—"

"It is his birthright," Mayday continued, interrupting Skye. "One thing we wolves hold dear is our family lines. The boy may be raised as a member of the Nightstar Pack, but once he is grown, we want to ensure he will have the right to decide if he will go back to his family's pack. It will be his choice and his alone to denounce his claim on the Blackmane."

Skye stared at Mayday. Shifted her eyes to the others. They all had the same unreadable gaze.

"But—"

"It's a win," Ricca murmured. She took Skye's arm and turned her to her. A smile ghosted her lips as she cupped Skye's cheek. "He stays with us now, and we will raise him to the best of our ability. When he is grown, it will be his right. We can only raise him to be a good man, and then he will go off on his own. He's ours."

Those last two words caused the waterworks to flow. Ricca and the council were right. Her son would have the right to know his father's people. She faced the council and inhaled sharply.

"I understand your decision and I am thankful my son can stay with me. At the age of eighteen, I will encourage him to follow his heart."

"We are grateful for the council taking time to hear us out." Ricca rested a hand on her shoulder.

"Please give our greetings to your alpha," Dowers said.

"Yes, sir. I will share with him your compassion." Ricca gave her a nod.

"But what about Barone? Who will keep him from coming after my son?" Skye asked. It was all well and good that they agreed with her, but who was going to keep that maniac in place?

"Don't worry, my dear. We will send official notice to the alpha of the Blackmane." Mayday came to stand in front of them with a wide grin spreading on his face. He took Skye's hand in his and patted the back of it. "When you leave here, go home knowing you and your family are safe."

Her family.

Skye returned his smile with one of her own and looked to Ricca.

"He won't be able to touch us," Ricca said. She jostled Rolf in her arms while patting his back. "And he won't be able to touch Rolf."

"Let's go home," Skye whispered. She was so filled with joy, she could barely contain her emotions. She didn't know if she was going to cry or laugh hysterically.

"Please escort them to their vehicle," Mayday called out to the guards standing behind them.

The two massive men at the door gave a nod and waited for them.

"Thank you again," Skye said.

"Good luck, my child. If you need anything

else, please don't hesitate to reach out to us," Linota encouraged.

"Don't worry about Barone. We will take care of him." Bosch's deep voice sent a chill down Skye's spine.

She wasn't sure what that meant and didn't want to. She just wanted to go back to Howling Valley and start her new life with Ricca.

CHAPTER FIFTEEN

The hairs on the back of Ricca's neck rose. She handed Rolf back to Skye because she had the sudden feeling she was going to need her hands or shift quickly. She didn't want to alert Skye, so she kept a smile on her lips and walked alongside her while they followed the two council guards out of the building.

She jogged down the stairs, and immediately her wolf slammed against her stomach.

Her animal sensed something was off, too.

She looked at the guards; they sensed danger as well.

Ricca's gaze roamed the area. It was eerily quiet outside, and still. The other guards who were posted outside jogged down the stairs and spread out, searching

"What's wrong?" Skye's voice shook.

Ricca cursed, hating that her mate was scared. Her wolf snarled, ready to protect their mate and child.

"I don't know, but whatever it is, they also sense it." Ricca gently positioned Skye at her back. She didn't want to take any chances.

It was then three oversized SUVs came racing down the street, headed toward the building.

"We have incoming," the largest guard growled.

The trucks came to a screeching halt about a hundred yards away. It was comforting to see the council guards surround her, Skye, and the baby.

Ricca braced herself. Her gums burned and stretched while her canines descended. The truck doors flew open. Ricca's gaze landed on the first figure, and the bottom of her stomach gave way.

Barone.

She recognized him from the video conference. He appeared even wilder in person. The mad alpha strode forward, barking a laugh.

"It would appear luck would be on my side tonight," he boasted. His gaze landed on her.

Ricca tried to stand taller. She wasn't afraid of him. She would defend her mate and child until she breathed no more.

"Skye," he demanded, "bring the boy to me."

"No!" Her mate moved from behind her and came to stand beside her.

Ricca had to admit she was proud of her mate. She knew how hard this must be for Skye. She'd run from this crazy man, fearing for her life and that of her child.

"You don't get to tell me no. Shifter law states the boy belongs with his pack."

Other men stepped from the trucks. Ricca's muscles tensed.

This wasn't going to go over easy.

"You need to return to your vehicle, Barone Westway of the Blackmane," Bosch's deep voice rang out.

Ricca didn't take her eyes off the alpha. She inhaled sharply and scented the members of the council.

"Not without my boy's son," Barone growled. He took a step forward and pointed at Skye. "That bitch is keeping my grandson from me. I have a right to that baby."

A movement from the corner of Ricca's eyes snagged her attention.

More council guards. She glanced around, and it was then she noticed the guards all had large daggers in their hands. They were massive and jagged.

Ricca was unsure of where they kept them, but it would appear the guards were ready for war. She had heard the council's guards were deadly, and tonight she was going to get front-row seats of them in action.

"We will ask you one more time, Alpha. Return to your vehicle." Markway's voice was eerily calm yet threatening.

"No one is keeping me from that baby." Barone bared his fangs. He took another step forward, ignoring the council guards. The crazed look in his eyes was dangerous. He was willing to go to war.

"He can't have my baby," Skye whispered.

"He won't," Ricca replied.

"Alpha, we have granted Ms. Lennon the right to keep her child with her," Estella stated.

Ricca tensed at the villainous snarl that erupted

from Barone. He shook his jacket off. Dark hair spread out along his arms.

Ricca cursed.

He was going to shift.

"You can't do that," he bit out around his fangs.

"We can and we have," Linota's voice sounded. "We, the council, have deemed this so. The child may stay with his mother, and on his eighteenth birthday, he will make his own choice."

"She's going to turn him against me just like she did my boy!" Barone stalked toward them with his men behind him.

The sound of clothing ripping and growls filled the air.

They were about to do this on council grounds.

Her animal prowled inside Ricca, waiting for the chance to break free.

"Go to the council." Ricca gently pushed Skye away from her and urged her on.

Skye didn't hesitate on following commands and jogged back up the stairs. Linota assisted her and pulled her to stand between her and Estella. Four other guards came from the building and stood with the council. Once she saw Skye and Rolf were safe with the council, Ricca turned back to sounds of fighting.

Barone's men were no match for the guards.

It was Barone she worried about. The strength of an alpha was unmatched to regular wolves.

Barone had fully shifted.

"Shit," Ricca muttered, watching the guards engage with Barone's wolves.

Her animal burst forward and slammed against her.

Ricca gave in, letting her beast out.

Her body contorted, clothes ripping and falling to the ground. Her fur sprouted on her arms, and within seconds she was standing on four paws. This had to be the quickest she'd ever shifted.

Her animal snarled. She flew forward and joined in on the fight. This was what she had trained for when she became an enforcer.

Protecting those who would need her.

Barone's growl caught her attention. She headed toward him while he fought viciously. She ran to aid the council guards as they surrounded him. His hard eyes landed on her, and he darted toward her. He was almost double her size with paws large enough to cover her face.

She wasn't afraid of him.

He was here to take Rolf.

The little boy was like her son. She and her

wolf loved him so, and she'd be damned if this deranged alpha was going to take him from her and Skye.

Ricca growled and narrowed her eyes on Barone.

One second he was racing toward her, and the next, four large guards crashed into him. She skidded to a halt in shock.

He snarled and tried to kick them off, but he was not successful.

A guard in his human form walked forward and placed a collar around his neck. Ricca was fascinated watching Barone continue to writhe on the ground and try to break free.

Right before her eyes, he shifted into his human form.

What the hell?

He fell back onto the ground and rolled over onto his stomach.

"What the fuck is this contraception?" he hollered.

"Barone Westway of the Blackmane pack, you are hereby placed under arrest." The guard's voice was inhumanly low.

Ricca glanced around and found the guards had bested the Blackmane pack. They were back in their human forms. Ricca looked at the alpha, pulling back on her animal. She stood, unable to believe she was witnessing this.

It was rare the council activated their powers over an alpha.

This was a big fucking deal.

"I am an alpha. You cannot arrest me." He stood to his full height, his chest rising and falling fast.

"We can. The proclamation of greater good law states that the council can overthrow an alpha who is no longer worthy of the title of alpha," Mayday said. Dowers joined him and stood in front of Barone. "You have been under investigation for some time, Westway."

"You can't strip me of my power!" Barone jerked forward but was held back by two of the council's guards.

"Westway, there is some disheartening information that has been reported to the council. You will be held and judged," Dowers announced.

Ricca's eyes grew wide. She knew the council had power, but she never thought she would see a day where they had stripped an alpha of his title. Most alphas either inherited their title from their fathers, were appointed by a pack, or they fought to win the title.

"We will name a replacement to stand in place until Rolf Westway is old enough to make the decision of claiming his birthright," Mayday said.

"You can't do this!" Barone shouted. Spittle flew from his mouth. The evil wolf tried to shift. His fur sprouted slightly on his arms then drew back in.

Fascinating.

The device around his neck was keeping him from shifting.

"Take him and his men away to the dungeon to stand trial." Dowers motioned to the building behind them.

The guards dragged away the dishonorably stripped alpha with his men. Ricca raced over to Skye who stood with the other members of the council. Tears streamed down her face.

"What it is, mate?" Ricca asked. She reached for Skye, not liking the sight of her tears. She should be happy Barone was being led away.

"It's over?" Skye asked.

"Yes, my dear." Linota turned to her. "Barone crossed the line by attacking the council. He will pay for his actions. Attacking the council is an absolute disrespect that cannot go unpunished. We will choose a temporary alpha of the Blackmane. We will leave Rolf's future into his hands."

Skye glanced down at their son and kissed his forehead.

"Any decision he will make, I will follow," Skye said. She glanced at Ricca and hesitated. "I mean, if that is okay with you."

"Of course, it is. Whatever our son decides, we will support. If he chooses to become alpha, then we will follow him." Ricca would share with Evan the decision of the council. He was a fair alpha, and if it meant being involved to mentor her son, she was sure he would. Evan was a great example of how an alpha should be.

"You two go home. We will take care of everything." Estella smiled at them. She reached out and tapped Rolf on the nose. "Take this little alpha home so he can get some rest."

"Yes, ma'am." Ricca nodded to them. She was grateful to the council. The future of her family was now secured. She turned to Skye and held out her hand. "Let's go home, mate."

"Yes, let's." Skye placed her hand in hers and smiled.

They walked toward their SUV in a comfortable silence, holding hands. Skye's eyes kept flicking to her while a small smile played on her lips.

"What is it, mate?" Ricca asked.

"Do you have an extra change of clothes? Or are you driving home like that?" Skye giggled.

The sound of it sent a warm rush of emotions through Ricca. She promised from this day forth, she would ensure Skye always had something to smile about. Ricca glanced down at her naked form and shrugged.

"I think I might have a shirt I can slip on." She winked at her mate, loving the dark blush spreading along her cheeks.

Skye skipped ahead, eliciting a squeal from Roth. Skye's hips swayed more, and she peeked over her shoulder.

"Then the trip home will be much more interesting." She wiggled two fingers playfully and ran ahead toward the truck.

Ricca paused in shock.

Her little mate never surprised her.

She grinned and followed behind the woman she loved. Yes, this trip home was going to be very interesting indeed.

EPILOGUE

The bond between mother and child was undeniable. Skye laughed, holding her hands out to Rolf. He was taking his first steps. The past five months had flown by, and she couldn't be any happier.

She was mated to the love of her life.

Once they had returned home from Aston, she and Rolf had moved in with Ricca.

"You made it!" she exclaimed, closing her arms around his little frame.

He had grown up so much. He was tall for his age and strong. As he had gotten older, he looked so much like Reade it made her heart ache. She wished he was here to see his son. He would be so proud. It was a wonder how someone like Reade came from someone like Barone.

"Mama." He grinned at her, showcasing two of his tiny fangs that had come in.

Skye's heart swelled so much with love for her child. He had started putting some words together. He was thriving wonderfully.

He loved outside, and each day before lunch, she took him outside to play. Some days they'd walk to the park or along the trails in the woods.

This was how life should be. No looking over her shoulder. No fear that at any moment her deranged father-in-law would be trying to take her child.

The sound of a vehicle pulling into the driveway captured her attention.

"Is that Mama?" she asked in a singsong voice.

She lifted him and walked around their home. Ricca had allowed her to redecorate to make the cabin feel more welcoming and to make sure it felt like a home for the both of them.

She saw Ricca's truck parked in the driveway. Skye's heart stuttered at the sight of her mate stepping from the truck. Her long silvery hair was braided into an intricate design that reminded Skye of a warrior's crown. A few strands escaped around her face.

"Look who it is." Skye turned Rolf around so he could see Ricca.

He fidgeted in her arms and raised his hands to Ricca.

"Hey, big boy!" Ricca grinned and rushed over to them.

Rolf dove into her arms with a squeal.

"Mama," he said. He reached for Ricca's cheeks.

She brought her head down and rested her forehead on his.

Skye sighed, loving the sight of her mate and child together. If she wasn't already in love with Ricca, she would be now.

"How's Mommy doing?" Ricca brought her in close. She pressed a soft kiss to Skye's lips.

Skye melted against Ricca. The glint in Ricca's eyes promised her more later.

"I'm okay." Skye stepped back slightly from Ricca.

They walked to the steps and took a seat.

Skye moved close to Ricca who was balancing

Rolf on her lap. "What are you doing home so early?"

"Well, there is news about Barone."

Skye stiffened. She tried to not think about him. She didn't want to ruin her happiness by memories of him.

But she couldn't act like he didn't exist. He was a part of her history and her son's. One day she would have to tell her son about his family and where he came from..

"What about him?

"Evan shared with me that they have officially stripped his title and pack. There were countless reports of his abuse to members of his pack. He did not honor the alpha code and he will pay for his crimes. He will be imprisoned in Purgatory for fifty years."

"What is Purgatory?" Skye asked.

"It's a prison designed for the supernatural." Ricca took Skye's hand and kissed it. "You are officially free of him and his tyranny."

Skye blinked back tears.

It was really over.

"That is amazing. But who did they appoint over the pack?"

"It would appear Barone had a younger brother

who agreed to be the temporary alpha until Rolf is of age."

"An uncle?" She racked her brains and faintly remembered Reade mentioning an uncle.

From what she recalled, his uncle and Barone didn't get along, and the uncle had strayed from the pack. If the council felt it was best to appoint this wolf to lead, then she trusted they knew best. She thought of all the innocents who had remained in the pack who were too afraid to leave. She hoped this would be a new beginning for them.

One day she would take her son back to Half Moon Bay so he could learn about his pack. She would not hide the truth from him at all. He needed to know his other family.

"I'm also home because I have a surprise." Ricca stood and rested Rolf on her hip.

"What is that?" Skye narrowed her gaze on her mate.

"Nothing crazy. I booked us a family photo with Mindi. She had a cancellation, and she can take us today."

"What?" Skye glanced down at herself. She was a mess. Taking care of an almost-one-year-old was time-consuming. Her shirt had something questionable on it, her leggings were on day two. She eyed

Ricca. Mindi's photos were world-renowned. Since Skye had settled in Howling Valley, Echo's shop had become one of her favorite places to frequent. She'd gotten to know the pair and considered them good friends.

"Don't worry, my love. Just grab a shower and pick out a cute outfit. Everything will be taken care of."

Skye stood and closed the gap between them. She rose on her tiptoes and pressed her lips to Ricca's. She didn't know what she would do without this woman.

"Do you know how much I love you?" She smiled.

Ricca pressed another kiss to her lips.

"You can show me later." Ricca winked. Another kiss. "And just for the record, I love you more."

Taming Her Mate is the next book in the Nightstar Shifters series, and is now available!

Want to stay updated on Ariel Marie's releases, sign up for her mailing list!

LETTER FROM THE AUTHOR

Dear Reader,

Thank you for taking the time to read my book! I hope you enjoyed reading Ricca and Skye's story. I had so much fun writing it and love these two!

I would like to give a personal thank you to the readers who have reached out to me to share with me how much they love this series. I'm blown away by all of the support and love for the Nightstar Shifters series. It means so much to me that readers are enjoying this series.

As always, if you want more from Howling

Valley and the Nightstar Shifter pack, leave a review telling me this!

Love,

Ariel Marie

Taming Her Mate

THE NIGHTSTAR SHIFTERS BOOK 6

Will the love of her witch be enough to heal her wolf?

Kardia Marway was sent to Howling Valley to live a peaceful life. As the granddaughter of a councilman, her life would always be in the spotlight and dangerous. She would be free to live as she wanted in her new town with her little secret.

Kardia couldn't shift.

Her wolf refused to make an appearance.

River Delacroix was a powerful witch and healer. The moment she laid her eyes on Kardia, she knew the wolf was in pain and needed her help.

She was desperate to help Kardia. Everything she tried failed. She had to succeed because she'd awakened for Kardia. This wolf was the other half of her soul.

If her love for the wolf shifter couldn't fix her, how could they truly seal their bond?

Grab your copy of Taming Her Mate (The Nightstar Shifters book 6) now!

Deadly Kiss

THE IMMORTAL REIGN 1

A vampire princess. A human. One drop of blood changed their lives forever.

Vampires had taken everything from Quinn Hogan during the war. She had spent her entire life hiding from them. The last thing Quinn wanted in life was to be matched to one. Each human was required by law to enter the draft. Her name was randomly picked for submitting her blood sample.

Chances of being chosen? A million to one.

Luck had never been on her side.

Quinn matched with a vampire.

Now she was being shipped off to some random vampire who would probably bleed her dry.

Velika Riskel didn't want a mate. As the warden of Northwest America, there was no time for her to take a mate. When the human arrived, she had planned to release her, but one look into Quinn's hazel eyes and all of that changed.

Velika and Quinn's relationship was doomed from the start. Velika was a seasoned warrior who wasn't afraid of challenges. The vampire princess was determined to win Quinn's heart, defend her against a rival, and then claim her.

Don't miss this sexy, FF vampire romance tale.
Grab your copy today!

Moon Valley Shifters

A FF WOLF SHIFTER BOXSET

Three steamy stories of female shifters finding the mate destined for them. If you love sexy as sin, F/F wolf shifters paranormal romance stories, that will leave you breathless, then grab this hot box set!

Book 1 Lyric's Mate

Lyric moved to Moon Valley for a fresh start. A new town, a new home, and a new job was a dream come true. Finding that her new boss was her mate was totally unexpected. Will she be able to keep her wolf at bay?

Book 2 Meadow's Mate

Meadow, the new teacher in town had her eyes on the only female enforcer in the pack. Little did she know, the enforcer had Meadow in her sights. When a group of rogue wolves blows into town, will Sage be able to save her?

Book 3 Tuesday's Mate

Tuesday, the new accountant in town was setting up her new business in Moon Valley. Tuesday is entranced by Sunni, the coffee shop owner. Their wolves know they are meant for each other. But will Sunni and Tuesday listen to their beasts?

WARNING: These stories are sexy, fast-paced and will leave you begging for more.

Want to hear more from this tantalizing book?
Grab your copy today!

ABOUT THE AUTHOR

Ariel Marie is an author who loves the paranormal, action and hot steamy romance. She combines all three in each and every one of her stories. For as long as she can remember, she has loved vampires, shifters and every creature you can think of. This even rolls over into her favorite movies. She loves a good action packed thriller! Throw a touch of the supernatural world in it and she's hooked!

She grew up in Cleveland, Ohio where she currently resides with her husband and three beautiful children.

For more information:
www.thearielmarie.com

Also by Ariel Marie

Blackclaw Alphas (Reverse Harem Series)

Fate of Four

Bearing Her Fate (TBD)

The Midnight Coven Brand

Forever Desired

Wicked Shadows

Paranormal Erotic Box Sets

Vampire Destiny (An Erotic Vampire Box Set)

Moon Valley Shifters Box Set (F/F Shifters)

The Dragon Curse Series (Ménage MFF Erotic Series)

The Dark Shadows Series

Princess

Toma

Phaelyn

Teague

Adrian

Nicu

Stand Alone Books

Dani's Return

A Faery's Kiss

Printed in the USA
CPSIA information can be obtained
at www.ICGtesting.com
JSHW020252071123
51572JS00002B/86

9 781956 602142